EL BRONX REMEMBERED

a novella and stories

EL BRONX REMEMBERED

a novella and stories

by Nicholasa Mohr

Arte Público Press

Houston

El Bronx Remembered, a novella and stories
Second Edition
ISBN 0-934770-62-X
Copyright © 1986 by Nicholasa Mohr
All rights reserved
Arte Público Press
University of Houston
University Park
Houston, Texas 77004

To the memory of my mother,
for those days of despair
when she shared her magic gift of storytelling,
making all things right.

CONTENTS

There have been Puerto Ricans living in the mainland U.S.A. since the middle of the last century. But it was after the second World War, when traveling became cheaper and easier, that the greatest influx began. In 1946, Puerto Ricans could purchase, for a small amount of money, a one-way ticket to the mainland. As citizens they did not face immigration laws or quotas . . . and so they arrived by the tens of thousands, first by freighter and later by airplane.

A small percentage went to work as migrant workers in the rural areas of the country. The majority settled in New York City. Many went to live in Spanish Harlem, known as El Barrio, an older community of Spanish-speaking people, on Manhattan's Upper East Side. There they joined family and friends. Others moved into congested neighborhoods in-habited by the children of earlier immigrant groups. Thus, they formed new neighborhoods in Brooklyn and Manhat-tan's Lower East Side. One area in particular was heavily populated by these newcomers, and became an extension or suburb of Spanish Harlem. This was the South Bronx, known to the Puerto Ricans as "El Bronx."

These migrants and their children, strangers in their own country, brought with them a different language, culture, and racial mixture. Like so many before them they hoped for a better life, a new future for their children, and a piece of that good life known as the "American dream."

This collection of stories is about the Puerto Rican mi-grants and their everyday struggle for survival, during that decade of the promised future 1946 through 1956, in New York City's "El Bronx."

Nicholasa Mohr

A VERY SPECIAL PET

The Fernández family kept two pets in their small five-room apartment. One was a large female alley cat who was a good mouser when she wasn't in heat. She was very large and had a rich coat of grey fur with black stripes and a long bushy tail. Her eyes were yellow and she had long white whiskers. Her name was Marialu.

If they would listen carefully to what Marialu said, Mrs. Fernández assured the children, they would hear her calling her husband Raúl.

"Raúl . . . Raúl . . . this is Marialu . . . Raúl . . . Raúl . . . this is Marialu," the children would sing loudly. They all felt sorry for Marialu, because no matter how long and hard she howled, or how many times she ran off, she could never find her real husband, Raúl.

The second pet was not really supposed to be a pet at all. She was a small, skinny white hen with a red crest and a yellow beak. Graciela and Eugenio Fernández had bought her two years ago, to provide them and their eight children with good fresh eggs.

Her name was Joncrofo, after Graciela Fernández's favorite Hollywood movie star, Joan Crawford. People would

1

repeat the hen's name as she pronounced it, "Joncrofo la gallina."

Joncrofo la gallina lived in the kitchen. She had one foot tied with a very long piece of twine to one of the legs of the kitchen sink. The twine was long enough for Joncrofo to wander all over the kitchen and even to hop onto the large window with the fire escape. Under the sink Mrs. Fernández kept clean newspapers, water, and cornmeal for the hen, and a wooden box lined with some soft flannel cloth and packing straw. It was there that they hoped Joncrofo would lay her eggs. The little hen slept and rested there, but perhaps because she was nervous, she had never once laid an egg.

Graciela and Eugenio Fernández had come to the Bronx six years ago and moved into the small apartment. Except for a trip once before to the seaport city of Mayagüez in Puerto Rico, they had never left their tiny village in the mountains. To finance their voyage to New York, Mr. and Mrs. Fernández had sold their small plot of land, the little livestock they had, and their wooden cabin. The sale had provided the fare and expenses for them and their five children. Since then, three more children had been born. City life was foreign to them, and they had to learn everything, even how to get on a subway and travel. Graciela Fernández had been terribly frightened at first of the underground trains, traffic, and large crowds of people. Although she finally adjusted, she still confined herself to the apartment and seldom went out.

She would never complain; she would pray at the small altar she had set up in the kitchen, light her candles and murmur that God would provide and not forget her and her family. She was proud of the fact that they did not have to ask for welfare or home relief, as so many other families did.

"Papi provides for us. We are lucky and we have to thank Jesus Christ," she would say, making the sign of the cross.

Eugenio Fernández had found a job as a porter in one of the large buildings in the garment center in Manhattan. He still held the same job, but he hoped to be promoted someday to freight-elevator operator. In the meantime, he sold newspapers and coffee on the side, ran errands for people in the building, and was always available for extra work. Still, the money he brought home was barely enough to support ten people.

"Someday I'm gonna get that job. I got my eye on it, and Mr. Friedlander, he likes me . . . so we gotta be patient. Besides the increase in salary, my God!—I could do a million things on the side, and we could make a lotta money. Why I could . . ." Mr. Fernández would tell his family this story several times a week.

"Oh, wow! Papi, we are gonna be rich when you get that job!" the children would shriek.

"Can we get a television when we get rich, Papi?" Pablito, the oldest boy, would ask. Nellie, Carmen, and Linda wanted a telephone.

"Everybody on the block got a telephone but us." Nellie, the oldest girl, would speak for them.

The younger children, William, Olgita, and Freddie, would request lots of toys and treats. Baby Nancy would smile and babble happily with everybody.

"We gonna get everything and we gonna leave El Bronx," Mr. Fernández would assure them. "We even gonna save enough to buy our farm in Puerto Rico—a big one! With

3

lots of land, maybe a hundred acres, and a chicken house, pigs, goats, even a cow. We can plant coffee and some sugar, and have all the fruit trees—mangoes, sweet oranges, everything!" Mr. Fernández would pause and tell the children all about the wonderful food they could eat back home in his village. "All you need to get the farm is a good start."

"We gonna take Joncrofo, right?" the kids would ask. "And Maríalu? Her too?"

"Sure," Mr. Fernández would say good-naturedly, "even Raúl, her husband, when she finds him, eh?" He would wink, laughing. "And Joncrofo don't have to be tied up like a prisoner no more—she could run loose."

It was the dream of Graciela and Eugenio Fernández to go back to their village as owners of their own farm, with the faith that the land would provide for them.

This morning Mrs. Fernández sat in her kitchen, thinking that things were just not going well. Now that the holidays were coming and Christmas would soon be here, money was scarcer than ever and prices were higher than ever. Things had been hard for Eugenio Fernández; he was still working as a porter and lately had been sick with a bad throat. They had not saved one cent toward their farm. In fact, they still owed the dry-goods salesman for the kitchen curtains and two bedspreads; even insurance payments were long overdue. She wanted to find a job and help out, but there were still three small preschool children at home to care for. Lately, she had begun to worry; it was hard to put meat on the table.

4

Graciela Fernández sighed, looking about her small, clean kitchen, and caught sight of Joncrofo running frantically after a stray cockroach. The hen quickly jerked her neck and snapped up the insect with her beak. In spite of all the fumigation and daily scrubbing, it seemed there was always a cockroach or two in sight. Joncrofo was always searching for a tasty morsel—spiders, ants, even houseflies. She was quick and usually got her victim.

The little white hen had a wicked temper and would snap at anyone she felt was annoying her. Even Maríalu knew better; she had a permanent scar on her right ear as a result of Joncrofo's sharp yellow beak. Now the cat carefully kept her distance.

In spite of Joncrofo's cantankerous ways, the children loved her. They were proud of her because no one else on the block had such a pet. Whenever other children teased them about not having a television, the Fernández children would remind them that Joncrofo was a very special pet. Even Baby Nancy would laugh and clap when she saw Joncrofo rushing toward one of her tiny victims.

For some time now, Mrs. Fernández had given up any hope of Joncrofo producing eggs and had also accepted her as a house pet. She had tried everything: warm milk, fresh grass from the park, relining the wooden box. She had even consulted the spiritualist and followed the instructions faithfully, giving the little hen certain herbs to eat and reciting the prayers; and yet nothing ever worked. She had even tried to fatten her up, but the more Joncrofo ate, it seemed, the less she gained.

After thinking about it for several days, this morning

5

Graciela Fernández reached her decision. Tonight, her husband would have good fresh chicken broth for his cold, and her children a full plate of rice with chicken. This silly hen was really no use alive to anyone, she concluded.

It had been six long years since Mrs. Fernández had killed a chicken, but she still remembered how. She was grateful that the older children were in school, and somehow she would find a way to keep the three younger ones at the other end of the apartment.

Very slowly she got up and found the kitchen cleaver. Feeling it with her thumb, she decided it should be sharper, and taking a flat stone, she carefully sharpened the edge as she planned the best way to finish off the hen.

It was still quite early. If she worked things right, she could be through by noontime and have supper ready before her husband got home. She would tell the children that Joncrofo flew away. Someone had untied the twine on her foot and when she opened the window to the fire escape to bring in the mop, Joncrofo flew out and disappeared. That's it, she said to herself, satisfied.

The cleaver was sharp enough and the small chopping block was set up on the kitchen sink. Mrs. Fernández bent down and looked Joncrofo right in the eye. The hen stared back without any fear or much interest. Good, thought Mrs. Fernández, and she walked back into the apartment where Olgita, Freddie, and Baby Nancy were playing.

"I'm going to clean the kitchen, and I don't want you to come inside. Understand?" The children looked at her and nodded. "I mean it—you stay here. If I catch you coming to the kitchen when I am cleaning, you get it with this,"

6

she said, holding out her hand with an open palm, gesturing as if she were spanking them. "Now, I'm going to put the chair across the kitchen entrance so that Baby Nancy can't come in. O.K.?" The children nodded again. Their mother very often put one of the kitchen chairs across the kitchen entrance so the baby could not come inside. "Now," she said, "you listen and you stay here!" The children began to play, interested only in their game.

Mrs. Fernández returned to the kitchen, smoothed down her hair, readjusted her apron, and rolled up her sleeves. She put one of the chairs across the threshold to block the entrance, then found a couple of extra rags and old newspapers.

"Joncrofo," she whispered and walked over to the hen. To her surprise, the hen ran under the sink and sat in her box. Mrs. Fernández bent down, but before she could grab her, Joncrofo jumped out of her box and slid behind one of the legs of the kitchen sink. She extended her hand and felt the hen's sharp beak nip one of her fingers. "Ave María!" she said, pulling away and putting the injured finger in her mouth. "O.K., you wanna play games. You dumb hen!"

She decided to untie the twine that was tied to the leg of the sink and then pull the hen toward her. Taking a large rag, she draped it over one hand and then, bending down once more, untied the twine and began to pull. Joncrofo resisted, and Mrs. Fernández pulled. Harder and harder she tugged and pulled, at the same time making sure she held the rag securely, so that she could protect herself against Joncrofo's sharp beak. Quickly she pulled, and

7

with one fast jerk of the twine, the hen was up in the air. Quickly Mrs. Fernández draped the rag over the hen. Frantically, Joncrofo began to cackle and jump, flapping her wings and snapping her beak. Mrs. Fernández found herself spinning as she struggled to hold on to Joncrofo, who kept wriggling and jumping. With great effort, Joncrofo got her head loose and sank her beak into Mrs. Fernández's arm. In an instant she released the hen.

Joncrofo ran around the kitchen cackling loudly, flapping her wings and ruffling her feathers. The hen kept an eye on Mrs. Fernández, who also watched her as she held on to her injured arm. White feathers were all over the kitchen; some still floated softly in the air.

Each time Mrs. Fernández went toward Joncrofo, she fled swiftly, cackling even louder and snapping wildly with her beak.

Mrs. Fernández remained still for a moment, then went over to the far end of the kitchen and grabbed a broom. Using the handle, she began to hit the hen, swatting her back and forth like a tennis ball. Joncrofo kept running and trying to dodge the blows, but Mrs. Fernández kept landing the broom each time. The hen began to lose her footing, and Mrs. Fernández vigorously swung the broom, hitting the small white hen until her cackles became softer and softer. Not able to stand any longer, Joncrofo wobbled, moving with slow jerky movements, and dropped to the floor. Mrs. Fernández let go of the broom and rushed over to the hen. Grabbing her by the neck, she lifted her into the air and spun her around a few times, dropping her on the floor. Near exhaustion, Mrs. Fernández could hear her own heavy breathing.

8

"Mami . . . Mamita. What are you doing to Joncrofo?" Turning, she saw Olgita, Freddie, and Baby Nancy staring at her wide-eyed. "Ma . . . Mami . . . what are you doing to Joncrofo?" they shouted and began to cry. In her excitement, Mrs. Fernández had forgotten completely about the children and the noise the hen had made.

"Oooo . . . is she dead?" Olgita cried, pointing. "Is she dead?" She began to whine.

"You killed Joncrofo, Mami! You killed her. She's dead." Freddie joined his sister, sobbing loudly. Baby Nancy watched her brother and sister and began to cry too. Shrieking, she threw herself on the floor in a tantrum.

"You killed her! You're bad, Mami. You're bad," screamed Olgita.

"Joncrofo . . . I want Joncrofo. . . ." Freddie sobbed. "I'm gonna tell Papi," he screamed, choking with tears.

"Me too! I'm gonna tell too," cried Olgita. "I'm telling Nellie, and she'll tell her teacher on you," she yelled.

Mrs. Fernández watched her children as they stood looking in at her, barricaded by the chair. Then she looked down at the floor where Joncrofo lay, perfectly still. Walking over to the chair, she removed it from the entrance, and before she could say anything, the children ran to the back of the apartment, still yelling and crying.

"Joncrofo. . . . We want Joncrofo. . . . You're bad . . . you're bad. . . ."

Mrs. Fernández felt completely helpless as she looked about her kitchen. What a mess! she thought. Things were overturned, and there were white feathers everywhere. Feeling the tears coming to her eyes, she sat down and began to cry quietly. What's the use now? She sighed and thought,

9

I should have taken her to the butcher. He would have done it for a small fee. Oh, this life, she said to herself, wiping her eyes. Now my children hate me. She remembered that when she was just about Olgita's age she was already helping her mother kill chickens and never thought much about slaughtering animals for food.

Graciela Fernández took a deep breath and began to wonder what she would do with Joncrofo now that she was dead. No use cooking her. They won't eat her, she thought, shaking her head. As she contemplated what was to be done, she heard a low grunt. Joncrofo was still alive!

Mrs. Fernández reached under the sink and pulled out the wooden box. She put the large rag into the box and placed the hen inside. Quickly she went over to a cabinet and took out an eyedropper, filling it with water. Then she forced open Joncrofo's beak and dropped some water inside. She put a washcloth into lukewarm water and washed down the hen, smoothing her feathers.

"Joncrofo," she cooed softly, "cro . . . cro . . . Joncrofita," and stroked the hen gently. The hen was still breathing, but her eyes were closed. Mrs. Fernández went over to the cupboard and pulled out a small bottle of rum that Mr. Fernández saved only for special occasions and for guests. She gave some to Joncrofo. The hen opened her eyes and shook her head, emitting a croaking sound.

"What a good little hen," said Mrs. Fernández. "That's right, come on . . . come, wake up, and I'll give you something special. How about if I get you some nice dried corn? . . . Come on." She continued to pet the hen and talk sweetly to her. Slowly, Joncrofo opened her beak and tried to cackle, and again she made a croaking sound. Blinking her eyes, she sat up in her box, ruffled her feathers, and managed a low soft cackle.

"Is she gonna live, Mami?" Mrs. Fernández turned and saw Olgita, Freddie, and Baby Nancy standing beside her.

"Of course she's going to live. What did you think I did, kill her? Tsk, tsk . . . did you really think that? You are all very silly children," she said, and shook her finger at them. They stared back at her with bewilderment, not speaking. "All that screaming at me was not nice." She went on, "I was only trying to save her. Joncrofo got very sick, and see?" She held up the eyedropper. "I had to help her get well. I had to catch her in order to cure her. Understand?"

Olgita and Freddie looked at each other and then at their mother.

"When I saw that she was getting sick, I had to catch her. She was running all around, jumping and going crazy. Yes." Mrs. Fernández opened her eyes and pointed to her head, making a circular movement with her right index finger. "She went cuckoo! If I didn't stop her, Joncrofo would have really killed herself," she said earnestly. "So I gave her some medicine—and now . . ."

"Is that why you got her drunk, Mami?" interrupted Olgita.

"What?" asked Mrs. Fernández.

"You gave her Papi's rum . . . in the eyedropper. We seen you," Freddie said. Olgita nodded.

"Well," Mrs. Fernández said, "that don't make her drunk. It . . . it . . . ah . . . just calms her down. Sometimes it's used like a medicine."

"And makes her happy again?" Olgita asked. "Like

11

Papi? He always gets happy when he drink some."

"Yes, that's right. You're right. To make Joncrofo happy again," Mrs. Fernández said.

"Why did she get sick, Mami, and go crazy?" asked Freddie.

"I don't know why. Those things just happen," Mrs. Fernández responded.

"Do them things happen on the farm in Puerto Rico?"

"That's right," she said. "Now let me be. I gotta finish cleaning here. Go on, go to the back of the house; take Baby Nancy . . . go on."

The children left the kitchen, and Mrs. Fernández barricaded the entrance once more. She picked up the box with Joncrofo, who sat quietly blinking, and shoved it under the sink. Then she put the cleaver and the chopping board away. Picking up the broom, she began to sweep the feathers and torn newspapers that were strewn all about the kitchen.

In the back of the apartment, where the children played, they could hear their mother singing a familiar song. It was about a beautiful island where the tall green palm trees swayed under a golden sky and the flowers were always in bloom.

A NEW WINDOW DISPLAY

On a cold, bleak Monday morning early in January, Hannibal and Joey walked along the avenue. They were on their way to school. But first, as usual, they stopped in front of the FUNERARIA ORTIZ and looked at the new window display. Sometimes the other kids would be there waiting, but this morning Hannibal and Joey were the first to arrive.

"Man," said Hannibal, "it sure is cold today. Maybe it'll snow."

"I hope so," said Joey. "A whole lotta snow, and we can build some forts. . . . Neat! Huh, Hannibal?"

Hannibal nodded and turned to look at the storefront. "They got a new one today, but it's an old man."

"Again?" Joey asked.

Every Monday, the funeral chapel had a new window display of color photographs showing the recently deceased from different angles, including close-ups. The inscription on every wreath was clearly visible. Hannibal pointed to a large photograph of an older man in a white-satin-lined coffin. His grey hair was neatly combed back, showing a receding hairline. His face was a dark orange, with a pinkish

13

red spot on each cheek, and his lips were a deep purple-red, pushed back into a fixed smile. His eyes were shut. He wore a dark-blue suit and a clean white shirt with a black tie. His hands were folded over the lower part of his chest. They appeared very pale in contrast to his face; almost a greyish white. He wore a plain gold wedding band.

"They got a new one?" someone asked. Hannibal and Joey turned and saw Ramona, Mary, and Casilda.

"Well?" asked Ramona.

"They got an old man," answered Hannibal.

Ramona and the two girls stepped up and looked inside the storefront window. "Again?" Ramona asked.

"Yeah, all they got is old mens," Mary said.

"This guy got a mess of flowers. Look at all them decorations," said Joey. "Let's start reading them, O.K., Hannibal? Or . . . maybe we should wait for Papo and Little Ray." Joey looked at Hannibal, waiting for him to make the final decision.

"He's late, man, and it's cold. I say we start reading," Hannibal replied.

"Maybe we should wait a little bit. You know Papo always has to bring his cousin to school. . . ." Ramona said.

"No!" Hannibal said. "Let's read now." He looked at Ramona defiantly. She shrugged her shoulders.

"To our dear departed—" Hannibal began to read the inscription on one of the wreaths.

"Wait!" Ramona interrupted. "You going first again. You went first the last time."

"I don't remember going first last time," Hannibal said.

"Oh, yes! Right? Ask anybody." Ramona looked at the two girls standing beside her. They both nodded silently. "What do you think, Joey? Do you think I went first before?"

"I don't remember. I don't think so," Joey replied quickly.

"You see?" Hannibal said to Ramona. "Now let me read!"

Ramona made a face and whispered something.

"What?" asked Hannibal. "What did you say, girl?"

"Nothing," Ramona said, sighing. "Go on."

"To our dear departed Uncle Felix," Hannibal read, "from his loving niece and husband and children, Rojelia and Esteban Martínez, Gilberto, María Patricia and Consuelo."

"Para un gran amigo," Joey read from another wreath. "Felix Umberto Cordero. De la familia Jiménez, 5013 Kelly Street, Bronx, New York."

"From your loving sister, María Elena Martínez and . . ." Ramona took the next turn. Then Mary and Casilda read. It usually went in that order unless Papo and Little Ray were there. Then the girls would be the last ones. Papo was a year younger than the others, and his little cousin was almost two years younger than Papo. Little Ray and his parents had arrived a few months ago from Puerto Rico. They always saved one inscription written in Spanish for him, because he read Spanish better than English.

The children finished reading all the inscriptions. "I guess they are real late, or they ain't coming. We better split or we are gonna be late," said Hannibal.

15

The group started once more toward school. They walked quickly, feeling the cold wind against their faces and bodies. They turned the corner of Prospect Avenue and headed down Longwood Avenue toward P.S. 39.

Except for a term in the second grade and once in the fourth grade, the group had been in the same classes since kindergarten. This term, they were all in the fifth grade except Papo, who was in the fourth. New in the group, he had become their friend when he moved to the Bronx about a year ago.

Little Ray was always with Papo, who had to look after him. In the four months since he had arrived, he had become the group's favorite. At first he had spoken no English, but now he was almost fluent. He spoke with an accent, which amused the other children, and he would get back at them by correcting their Spanish.

"That's not the way you say it." Little Ray would smile and gently correct them, giving them the proper pronunciation. They would laugh at him, but they could not help being impressed with his ability to speak so well.

"Man . . . Little Ray talks Spanish as good as my grandmother and parents and everybody!" Joey had said.

"Yeah," Ramona agreed. "He sure knows a lot for such a little kid."

The group had become protective of Little Ray, and they soon included him in everything they did. They were always anxious to see and hear his reaction to something different, or new, that he had never seen before.

"Qué fenomenal!" Little Ray would always shout with excitement. Everyone laughed and giggled. After a while, it got to be a game; they would wait for Little Ray to

16

react, and then in unison they echoed, "Phenomenal!"

It was Little Ray's favorite word.

"He may be little but he's got a lotta heart, man. He's phenomenal! . . . And no squealer either," Hannibal had said admiringly, the day that they had all decided to take some potatoes from the vegetable stand in the outdoor market on Union Avenue.

Little Ray and Casilda were assigned to keep the man at the stand busy while the rest of them stuffed their pockets with roasting potatoes. Later, in an empty lot, they skewered the potatoes on long, thin pieces of wood, roasting them over an open fire, waiting for the skin to turn black and the inside soft and hot.

As they ate, a superintendent from one of the nearby tenements came over and began to question Little Ray suspiciously in Spanish. He assured the man, speaking to him in Spanish, that they had all brought the potatoes with them from home. After the man left, they laughed.

"He's the best little kid in El Bronx!" Ramona had said. "Right?"

"Phenomenal!" everyone had shouted in agreement.

Hannibal and Joey rushed on ahead, almost running, and left the girls a few yards behind.

"What do you mean the most flowers?" Hannibal argued with Joey.

"Yeah . . . today that man had the most decorations I seen so far."

"Get out, Joey. Remember the old lady with the wig that time? And the little baby—remember him? Now he had like a hundred decorations."

"Oh yeah, that's right," said Joey. "Do you think that was a real baby?"

"Of course it was! What do you think it was, a dummy?"

"No, but maybe . . . it was like a doll," Joey said.

"It was no doll. Man, Joey, what's the matter with you? Why they gonna give all them flowers to a doll and everything?"

"Well," Joey said. "Anyway, that was no hundred decorations he had. Wasn't even fifty!"

"Well, maybe not a whole hundred. But it was more than fifty and more than that old guy today got. . . ." Hannibal continued trying to convince Joey as they raced to reach school before the late bell rang.

"To Our Dear Departed Brother and Uncle, Carlos Rodríguez . . ." read Hannibal.

"Rest in Peace, Co-Worker. From . . ." read Joey. As usual, they all stood together looking at another new window display. This Monday morning, the weather was quite pleasant, unseasonably warm; and the sun shone brightly. Then it was Papo's turn.

"I'm gonna read the one in Spanish for Little Ray, even though he ain't here today," Papo said. "Querido Esposo, Padre, y Abuelo . . ." he finished reading.

"This guy didn't have so many decorations," said Casilda.

"Yeah, not like the last guy," Joey said. "Look, even the coffin ain't so fancy."

"Yeah."

"Uh huh."

"That's right."

18

"How is Little Ray?" asked Hannibal. "He ain't been around now for about almost two weeks, right?"

"Yeah . . . well," Papo answered, "I think he's gotta go back to P.R."

"Puerto Rico?" asked Joey. "No kidding?"

"He got something in his chest, like—and they say it's the bad weather here that causes it. It's real bad and he's very sick. They say he gotta go back."

"Aww man, that's too bad!" said Hannibal.

"That's terrible," said Mary.

"When does he gotta leave?" asked Ramona.

"As soon as he gets better, so he can travel," answered Papo. "And he don't like the idea at all, let me tell you. Little Ray says they are very strict down there and that here he is much more free. He likes to hang out with us and play and everything."

"Do you think, Papo, that if he gets really well and all better, that maybe they will let him stay here?" asked Ramona.

"I don't know." Papo shrugged his shoulders. "His parents definitely say he gotta go back and stay with his aunt and uncle down there."

"Too bad," said Casilda. "He's nice."

"He's a real good kid," Hannibal agreed.

"Yeah."

"Uh huh."

The mildness in the air and the bright sun put the children in high spirits. They all walked to school at a slow pace, enjoying the January thaw.

"What a drag," Hannibal said; "going to school on such

19

a day. It feels like springtime. How about cutting today?"

"Get out, Hannibal!" Ramona said quickly. "You better not start that business again and get into trouble. And you better not listen to him, Joey."

"Goody Two-Shoes," Hannibal said, making a face at Ramona.

Ramona stuck her tongue out at Hannibal.

"Whew . . . qué fea . . ." he said good-naturedly. "Ugly as sin." Ramona responded by shrugging her shoulders. Neither of them could really feel angry this morning.

The group strolled along and turned the corner onto Longwood Avenue.

"Hey . . . maybe if the weather changes and it keeps on being warm, they will let Little Ray stay. Then he can come back to school and stick around with us," said Joey.

"I sure hope so," said Papo, smiling. "Except after he gets well, then I hope it snows. He's never really seen snow—he's only seen like a little bit. Like flurries, so far. But I mean a real big storm. This way we could all build a fort, and have snowball fights and everything, you know. . . ."

"Yeah," said Mary, "that's right. Remember, we told Little Ray all about it. He was looking forward to it."

"Right now, let's just hope it stays warm," said Ramona. "That way he can come back and be with us real soon."

"Sure."

"Right."

"Absolutely."

A whole month had passed since Little Ray was buried. Many neighbors had attended the funeral mass. The group did not go, except for Papo. However, the members of the group had gone once to the funeral chapel with their families to pay their respects to Little Ray and his family. By now, things had gone back to normal except that the children no longer met in front of the storefront window of the FUNERARIA ORTIZ on Monday mornings. They just walked past the new window display on their way to school, not looking or stopping. No one ever spoke about it.

This morning, wet snow melted instantly as it hit the concrete pavement and black-tar streets. Hannibal and Joey rushed to school feeling cold and damp. As they approached the funeral chapel, they saw Papo, Ramona, Mary, and Casilda standing right in front of the storefront window.

"Hannibal, Joey—look!" Ramona called out, pointing to the new window display. "Papo told us."

Hannibal and Joey looked inside the storefront window and saw many photographs of Little Ray. There were so many floral wreaths that the small coffin was hardly visible. A large close-up showed him in a powder-blue, silk-lined coffin. His dark curly hair was oiled, combed and parted on the side. Little Ray's eyes were shut and his face was colored a light pink. Each cheek had a dark pink spot. His lips were bright orange and slightly parted. He looked like he was smiling, dreaming a pleasant dream. He wore his dark-blue First Holy Communion suit, with a white satin sash tied on his left sleeve, a white starched shirt, and a dark-blue tie. His small pale hands held a white missal and a set of white rosary beads with a gold cross.

"I thought we should stop. . . ." Papo hesitated. "My

21

parents told me last night, and I figured that it would only be right . . . for us to come here. For Little Ray."

The group remained silent for a while.

"Wow!" Hannibal said, breaking the silence. "He sure looks different, don't he?"

"Yeah," Joey said. "I never even seen him with his hair combed before. He even looks healthy, like he got a sunburn."

"My father says they do a good job here," said Papo, nodding. "They made him look like he was making his Communion again. They made everything perfect."

"He looks nice," Mary said.

"Oh . . . yeah, he does," said Casilda. "Like a little angel. Right?"

"He sure does." Ramona nodded.

"Now," Hannibal said. "He's the one that got the most flowers of anybody I ever seen!"

"That's right!" said Joey. "Even more than that little baby."

"Uh huh."

"The most!"

"Absolutely."

The children stood quietly and looked into the storefront window. The wet snow continued to fall. They were all damp and chilly, but no one moved. After a while, Papo asked, "Do you think we should read?"

The children looked at each other and shrugged. Then everyone turned to look at Hannibal.

"O.K.," Hannibal said, "who's gonna go first?" Everyone

22

was surprised. Hannibal had never asked anyone to be first before.

"You go first," said Ramona. "Like you always do." Hannibal opened his mouth to protest, but Ramona stared at him and, folding her arms, said quickly, "Go on!" Hannibal read slowly.

"To the Santiago family in their Hour of Bereavement . . ." He read on, looking at Joey when he finished.

"Beloved Son, Ramon Luis . . ." Joey read.

Each took a turn. There were so many wreaths that they went twice around, and Hannibal and Joey had to read a third time. Finally they were all finished.

"I still miss him, you know," Papo said. "I never even minded taking care of him . . . like he was no bother. Other little kids, man, you know, they can really be pests. But not him."

"He was really a good kid," said Hannibal.

"It's kinda funny, because like I know he's not gonna be around no more, yet like I can't believe he's gone." Papo paused for a moment, then continued, "Anyway, my parents ordered some of them pictures and this way we can remember him like he looked."

They walked silently toward school. It began to snow harder, and large snowflakes stuck to the pavement, piling up. Areas of sidewalk were covered by a soft white blanket. The children felt the soft crunch under their feet, so different from the familiar hard concrete.

"Hey!" yelled Joey. "We got us a real big snowstorm!"

"Hurray!"

The group shouted, sliding and turning.

"Oh, boy, imagine if Little Ray were here and seen this!" said Papo excitedly.

"Oh man! He would be so happy!" Hannibal smiled. "And we all know what he would say. . . ."

"Phenomenal!" everyone shouted.

"TELL THE TRUTH. . . ."

Vickie had been waiting in the reception room for almost one hour. Except for the thin lady who sat typing behind the desk opposite her, no one else was present. Once more, Vickie reread the name on the large dark-wood door. THEODORE M. CRANE, ESQ., ATTORNEY-AT-LAW was printed in gold with a black outline. The man inside that room behind the large door was her mother's lawyer. He had been retained by the people her mother worked for. Mr. Crane was supposed to tell her when she could see her mother again.

The telephone rang and the thin lady spoke softly. "She's right here. . . . Certainly, Mr. Crane." She put down the receiver and continued to type.

The door opened and Vickie saw Mr. Crane standing in the doorway. He beckoned to her and she followed him into a large room furnished with a black leather couch, two matching armchairs, and a large dark mahogany desk. The walls had wood paneling and bookshelves lined with law books. Many framed diplomas and certificates bearing his name and title were displayed on the wall.

He pointed to one of the armchairs in front of the desk, and Vickie quickly and obediently sat down.

She sat on the edge of the chair so that her feet could touch the floor. Vickie felt the soft carpeting under her shoes. Being able to touch the floor made her feel more secure. She was quite small for her age. She was thirteen, but people often thought she was younger.

Mr. Crane came over and bent down, patting Vickie on the shoulder a few times. He sighed deeply and then sat on the edge of his desk, facing her. She became aware of a dryness in her throat, and of the saliva that was quickly gathering in her mouth. Suddenly, it seemed she could not swallow. In panic, she looked all around the large office wondering where she could spit.

Mr. Crane looked down at her and smiled. With tremendous effort, Vickie swallowed, gulping down the saliva, and felt a sense of calm returning. Good, she thought, now if I can just hold down the spit, I'll be all right.

"Well," Mr. Crane said, and picked up a folder from his desk. He looked over the contents, then put it back. "You want to help your mother, don't you?" he asked. Vickie nodded. "Good. That's what this is all about, to help your mother." He smiled again.

Vickie wanted to ask him when she could see her mother, but she didn't dare to interrupt, so she waited to hear what Mr. Crane would say.

"You know, Victoria . . . Now that's a beautiful name. Victoria! And a famous one. You know, Queen Victoria. She was queen of the entire British Empire. And Victoria Falls. That's a famous waterfall in Africa. Did you know that? Well, then, Victoria, we are relying on you for the truth. For your mother's sake, you must tell us what

26

was going on, what really happened. Now . . . I'm going to ask you sincerely and honestly . . . so that you may help your mother. . . ." Mr. Crane hesitated. "Listen to me. Your mother deals in the numbers. Isn't that the truth? What you people call 'The Bolita'?" Mr. Crane stopped speaking and waited for her to respond.

". . . Not a word, Vickie, not a word . . . no matter what they ask, or who may talk to you. You don't know nothing! We don't know nothing. Remember!" Vickie could still hear her mother's voice speaking out to her in Spanish. She had returned from the movies on an afternoon three days ago to find her mother handcuffed, surrounded by detectives, and her little sisters and brother waiting in the kitchen. ". . . Not a word. This is a frame-up! The people I work for . . . they want to use me. It's serious. Don't say anything." Her mother's voice, loud and clear, still echoed in her head. Even as the detective led her out of the apartment, her mother called out, ". . . Nothing! Not one word to anyone. God bless you and . . ."

"Well?" Mr. Crane asked, looking at Vickie. She could feel her face flush in embarrassment as she shrugged her shoulders. "Victoria, you must tell the truth," he continued. "Doesn't your mother work for some bad people? Who make her sell drugs? Now, we know she's not the bad one. It's the others who are bad. Look here. . . . I don't mean the numbers; we know all about that. In fact"—his voice softened to a whisper—"these are the nice people who want to help your mother. They are the ones who want to take care of her." He paused, sighing, and spoke in a

27

loud tone. "Everyone knows what your mother does, and that's not important. . . . But if you tell me the truth about the drugs and let me know who some of these bad people are, it will help your mother. Make it easier on her. Understand?"

Vickie looked down at the floor, not speaking or moving.

"Answer me, please. Your mother is the one who is going to get into serious trouble unless we know the absolute truth about the drugs, so we can help her. Now, I have been retained as the family lawyer and it is my responsibility . . ." Mr. Crane kept his voice low and intimate. In a friendly manner, he continued to speak. "You know, after all, Vickie, I have kids of my own. I wouldn't ask you to do anything wrong. You must believe that."

The saliva gathered in her mouth once more, and she tried hard to swallow. It won't go down, she said to herself, frightened that the watery mess would begin to drip out of the sides of her mouth. Again, with great effort and concentration, she pushed hard. For a split second Vickie felt that she might choke, but instead managed to swallow and breathe. A close call! she thought.

". . . for instance, cómo estás?" Mr. Crane laughed softly. "See, how's that? I love Spanish, and I love your country. My family and I were in San Juan last winter. What an Island of Paradise! You should be proud of your country, Victoria. I know many, many Puerto Ricans. They visit us and we visit them. . . ."

Vickie and her younger sisters and brother were born in New York and had seldom left the Bronx. Every morning in school they pledged allegiance "to the flag of the United

28

States of America, and to the Republic for which it stands." She had never thought of Puerto Rico as her country. As Mr. Crane spoke, she remembered all the pictures of Puerto Rico she had seen in the Spanish magazines that her mother and Aunt Josefina read. "When I make a killing on the bolita—a big hit—" her mother had promised them, "I am taking you all on a trip to Santurce to meet your cousins, aunts and uncles." Although this had been the second arrest since her mother had been a numbers runner, things had been much better for them in the past two years. They were no longer on welfare and always had plenty of food and clothes. Except for the pressure not to open the door to anyone or discuss what their mother did with anybody, every day living seemed easier. Only Titi Josefina and her husband Paco could come and go as they pleased in the apartment. They lived in the next building and were close to Vickie and her little sisters and brother. No one else was allowed in the apartment. Not even school friends. A vague memory of her father remained. He had gone back to Puerto Rico.

". . . We want to help you, and your sisters and little brother. Believe me, I am your friend!" As Mr. Crane spoke, his voice became louder and held a note of irritation. "Victoria, please look at me when I speak to you. Don't look away! I'm trying to tell you something for your own good. Now please listen to me. Those people are trying to . . ."

Vickie had always been taught that children never looked directly at adults when they spoke, but rather lowered their eyes as a sign of respect. Now she was afraid not to look at Mr. Crane, so she observed him carefully. He had a full

29

head of grey hair, neatly trimmed and combed. His face was clean-shaven, almost looking benevolent. Like Santa Claus without no beard, Vickie said to herself. Except for his eyes; when she looked at his eyes, behind the thick lenses of his rimless glasses, they appeared distorted and strange.

He was dressed in a light-grey suit and a crisp white shirt and wore highly polished shoes. She concentrated on a tiny red-blue-and-green geometric design that covered his dark-blue socks. It looked like a tiny maze, and Vickie played a game, as he spoke, finding several ways in and out of the zigzag pattern.

"It's no longer a question of numbers, you know that? Drugs are involved now. That's right, drugs! Your mother will be involved unless she comes clean." Mr. Crane was almost shouting by now. His face had become a deep pink, and he waved his hands. They were a whitish-grey, and the nails had a coat of clear polish. Just as shiny as his shoes, Vickie said to herself. "Come on, Victoria. There are witnesses that can say your mother had drugs in the apartment. Don't try to deny this." He stopped shouting and lowered his voice. "Why don't you make it easier for your mother? I'll tell you what: Just admit that you saw that package in the house. The one containing that white powder . . . wrapped up in a plastic bag. . . . That's all you have to do, nothing else. Just so we get that cleared up, and everything will be easier for her." Mr. Crane folded his hands and waited. After a moment of silence, he asked, "Well?"

Vickie felt the saliva once more. Her mouth was so full she could hardly move her tongue. Opening her mouth, she took a breath and swallowed. "I don't know," she said.

Mr. Crane stood up and walked slowly around the room, coming back once more to where she was. "You must tell the truth and save your mother!" he shouted. Vickie looked at the floor and quietly shrugged her shoulders; she felt herself trembling, unable to speak.

"You don't want to be the one responsible for your mother's trouble, do you? You will send her to jail for twenty years! Do you want that? Do you? Answer!"

"No," she said. Vickie could still hear her mother's warning in Spanish. "Remember, they put that package here themselves to harm me. You must not say a word about anything! No matter who asks you. These people will frame me. Talk to no one, Vickie!"

"Well, then. Speak up. I want to hear you. Right now! Let me hear what you have to say."

"I don't know nothing. I can't tell you nothing. I don't know nothing about no numbers or drugs or nothing like that. At all." Vickie's voice was shaking, but she spoke clearly and deliberately. "Me and my kid sisters and little brother, we don't know nothing. There's nothing I can tell you about anything. I don't know nothing . . ."

"Stand up!" Mr. Crane interrupted. She stood up, wondering if she would be arrested. "How old are you?" he asked.

"Thirteen."

"You ought to be ashamed. Ashamed! You call yourself a young lady? I wouldn't be proud to call you my—" The telephone rang and Mr. Crane stopped speaking and picked up the receiver.

"Hello. Crane here." He waited a moment and then spoke

31

in a very low voice. "No, not a thing either. She won't co-operate. The kid is tight-lipped. . . . You know how these people are. . . . She's not about to say anything. . . . The package is insufficient. . . . Not without help. . . . Couldn't get anything here. There's not enough to hold her. No . . . no, that's right. They'll have to let her go. No. Under the circumstances I can't plea bargain. This will have to go as a misdemeanor. . . . Look, there's nothing I can do. We'll have to look for someone else. . . . All right then. All right, bring her here. Good-bye." Without looking at Vickie, he said, "Wait outside."

Vickie was not sure that he was speaking to her, so she didn't dare move. "I said wait outside. Now, go on!" Vickie looked at Mr. Crane; he had his back to her. She wanted to ask him when she could see her mother. But when she opened her mouth, she heard herself say, "Thank you."

Mr. Crane did not respond. Quietly and swiftly, Vickie opened the door and stepped into the reception room.

"All right," she heard the thin lady say. "Your mother will be here very soon." Vickie's heart jumped. "My mother?" she asked.

The thin lady nodded, and without looking up said, "Just stay seated and be patient. Read a magazine. She'll be right here, shortly."

Vickie felt herself shaking with joy. Her mother would be here very soon. After a short while, she realized with great relief that she could swallow again. Taking a deep breath, she picked up a magazine and began to read and look at the pictures.

Before she could finish the article, the outside door

opened, and Vickie saw her mother enter. She went toward Vickie with her arms outstretched. They embraced, and her mother asked her how she and the other children were.

The thin lady called in to Mr. Crane, and he came out to greet them. He smiled and shook hands with her mother.

"You have a fine girl there, Mrs. Vargas," he said.

"I know that," said Mrs. Vargas, hugging Vickie.

Without looking in Vickie's direction, Mr. Crane disappeared as he shut the door to his office.

The thin lady continued her typing and raised her arm in a gesture of good-bye.

Outside, in the street, Vickie said, "Mami, I didn't say one word. Not one word, just like you told me." Her mother stopped walking and with a big smile looked at her daughter.

"I know. . . . I know," she said happily. And they walked along with their arms around each other, heading for the subway and the long ride home to the Bronx.

SHOES FOR HECTOR

Hector's mother had gone to see Uncle Luis the day before graduation, and he had come by the same evening. Everyone sat in the living room watching Uncle Luis as he took a white box out of a brown paper bag. Opening the box, he removed a pair of shiny, light-caramel-colored shoes with tall heels and narrow, pointed toes. Holding them up proudly, he said, "Set me back twelve bucks, boy!"

Everyone looked at Hector and then back at Uncle Luis.

"Here you go, my boy. . . ." He gestured toward Hector. "Try them on."

"I'm not gonna try those things on!" Hector said.

"Why not?" asked Uncle Luis. "What's wrong with them? They are the latest style, man. Listen, boy, you will be a la moda with these."

"They . . . they're just not my type. Besides, they don't go with my suit—it's navy blue. Those shoes are orange!" Hector's younger brothers and sister looked at each other and began to giggle and laugh.

"Shut up, you dummies!" Hector shouted angrily.

"Hector, what is the matter with you?" his mother asked. "That's no way to behave."

"I'd rather wear my sneakers than those, Mami. You and

Papi promised to buy me shoes. You didn't say nothing about wearing Uncle Luis's shoes."

"Wait a minute, now. Just a minute," Hector's father said. "We know, but we just couldn't manage it now. Since your Uncle Luis has the same size foot like you, and he was nice enough to lend you his new shoes, what's the difference? We done what we could, son; you have to be satisfied."

Hector felt the blood rushing to his face and tried to control his embarrassment and anger. His parents had been preparing his graduation party now for more than a week. They should have spent the money on my shoes instead of on a dumb party, he thought. Hector had used up all the earnings from his part-time job. He had bought his suit, tie, shirt, socks, and handkerchief. His parents had promised to buy him the shoes. Not one cent left, he thought, and it was just too late now.

"It's not my fault that they lay me off for three days," his father said, "and that Petie got sick and that Georgie needed a winter jacket and Juanito some . . ."

As his father spoke, Hector wanted to say a few things. Like, No, it's my fault that you have to spend the money for shoes on a party and a cake and everything to impress the neighbors and the familia. Stupid dinner! But instead he remained quiet, looking down at the floor, and did not say a word.

"Hector . . . come on, my son. Hector, try them on, bendito. Uncle Luis was nice enough to bring them," he heard his mother plead. "Please, for me."

"Maybe I can get into Papi's shoes," Hector answered.

"My shoes don't fit you. And your brothers are all younger and smaller than you. There's nobody else. You

35

are lucky Uncle Luis has the same size foot," his father responded.

"O.K., I'll just wear my sneakers," said Hector.

"Oh, no . . . no, never mind. You don't wear no sneakers, so that people can call us a bunch of jíbaros! You wear them shoes!" his mother said.

"Mami, they are orange!" Hector responded. "And look at them pointed fronts—they go on for a mile. I'm not wearing them."

"Come on, please," his mother coaxed. "They look nice and brand new, too."

"Hector!" his father said loudly. "Now, your Uncle Luis was nice enough to bring them, and you are going to try them on." Everyone was silent and Hector sat sulking. His mother took the shoes from Uncle Luis and went over to Hector.

"Here, son, try them on, at least. See?" She held them up. "Look at them. They are not orange, just a light-brown color, that's all. Only a very light brown."

Without looking at anyone, Hector took the shoes and slowly put them on. No doubt about it, they felt like a perfect fit.

"How about that?" Uncle Luis smiled. "Now you look sharp. Right in style, boy!"

Hector stood up and walked a few paces. He knew what the kids called these shoes; he could hear them. "Roach killers. Man, the greenhorns wear them shoes to attack the cockroaches that hide in the corners. Man, they go right in there with them points and zap . . . zap . . . and snap . . . they're dead! Mata-cucaracha shoes." In spite of all the smiling faces in the living room, Hector still heard all the remarks he was sure his friends would make if he wore those shoes.

"O.K., you look wonderful. And it's only for one morning. You can take them right off after graduation," his mother said gently.

Hector removed the shoes and put them back in the box, resigned that there was just no way out. At that moment he even found himself wishing that he had not been selected as valedictorian and wasn't receiving any honors.

"Take your time, Hector. You don't have to give them back to me right away. Wear the shoes for the party. So you look good," he heard Uncle Luis calling out as he walked into his bedroom.

"Damn that stupid party!" Hector whispered out loud.

With a pained expression on his face the next morning, Hector left his apartment wearing Uncle Luis's shoes. His mother and father walked proudly with him.

Hector arrived at the school auditorium and took his place on line. Smiling and waving at him, his parents sat in the audience.

"Hector López . . ." He walked up the long aisle onto the stage. He finished his speech and sat on a chair provided for him on the stage. They called his name again several times, and each time Hector received an honor or prize. Included were a wristwatch and a check for cash. Whenever Hector stood up and walked to the podium, he prayed that no one would notice his shoes.

Finally, graduation exercises were over and Hector hurried off the stage, looking for his parents. People stopped him and congratulated him on his many honors and on his speech. His school friends shook his hand and they exchanged addresses. Hector found himself engaged in long good-byes. Slowly, people began to leave the large auditorium, and Hector and his parents headed for home.

Hector sat on his bed and took off Uncle Luis's shoes. "Good-bye," he said out loud, making a face, and dropped them into the box. He sighed with relief. No one had even mentioned the shoes, he thought. Man . . . I bet they didn't even notice them. Boy! Was I ever lucky. . . . Nobody said a word. How about that? he said to himself. Reaching under the bed, he took out his sneakers and happily put them on. Never again, he continued, if I can help it. No, sir. I'm gonna make sure I got me shoes to wear! He remembered all the things he had won at graduation. Looking at his new wristwatch, he put it on. That's really something, he thought. He took out the check for cash he had received and read, *"Pay to the Order of Hector López . . . The Sum of Twenty-Five Dollars and 00/100 Cents."* I can't wait to show everybody, he said to himself.

Hector left his room and looked into the kitchen. His mother and grandmother were busily preparing more food. He heard voices and music in the living room and quickly walked in that direction. When his younger brothers and sister saw him, they jumped up and down.

"Here's Hector!" Petie yelled.

"Happy Graduation Day, Hector!" everyone shouted.

The living room was full of people. His father was talking to Uncle Luis and some neighbors. Uncle Luis called out, "There he is. Hector! . . . There's my man now."

"Look." Hector's father pointed to a table that was loaded with platters of food and a large cake. The cake had the

38

inscription "Happy Graduation to Hector." Behind the cake was a large placard printed in bright colors:

HAPPY GRADUATION DAY, HECTOR
FROM ALL YOUR FAMILY
Mami, Papi, Abuelita, Petie, Georgie,
Juanito, and Millie

Rows of multi-colored crepe-paper streamers were strung across the ceiling and walls. Lots of balloons had been blown up and attached to each streamer. A big bell made of bright-red crepe paper and cardboard was set up under the center ceiling light. The record player was going full blast with a loud marengüe; some of the kids were busy dancing. Hector's face flushed when he saw Gloria. He had hoped she would come to the party, and there she was. Looking great, he thought.

Some neighbors came over and congratulated Hector. His friends began to gather around, asking him lots of questions and admiring his wristwatch.

"Show them the check, Hector," his father said proudly. "That's some smart boy; he just kept getting honors! Imagine, they even give him money. . . ."

Hector reached into his jacket pocket and took out the check for twenty-five dollars. He passed it around so that everyone could see it. Impressed, they asked him, "Hey, man. Hector, what you gonna do with all that money?"

"Yeah. Tell us, Hector, what you gonna do?"

Hector smiled and shrugged his shoulders. "Buy me a pair of shoes! Any color except orange!" he replied.

"ONCE UPON A TIME . . ."

Bouncey, bouncey, bally,
My sister's name is Paulie.
She gave me a smack,
I gave her one back.
Bouncey, bouncey, bally.

"Now it's my turn," said another girl. "Give me the ball." She too bounced the ball on the black tar roof of the tenement, throwing her right leg over the ball every third bounce.

One, two, three a nation
I received my confirmation
On the Day of Decoration
Just before my graduation.
One, two, three a nation!

"Me now," said the third girl, and took the Spalding ball, bouncing it the same way.

Once upon a time
A baby found a dime.
The dime turned red,
And the baby fell down dead!

40

"Me again," said the first girl and, taking the ball, began, "Bouncey, bouncey, bally, My sister's name is . . ."

After she finished, she handed the ball to the second girl, and then the third girl took a turn. They repeated this a few times and decided to stop playing.

"It's too hot up here," said the first girl. "Look, the tar is melting and getting stuck to my shoes."

"Ugh, yeah."

"Let's go."

They walked along the rooftops, going from building to building. Each building was separated from the next by a short wall of painted cement, stretching across the width of the building, no higher than three and a half feet. When they reached each wall the girls climbed over, exploring another rooftop.

"It's too hot out here; let's find a hallway to play in," said the second girl.

"O.K.," agreed the third girl, "but let's get a place where they don't throw us out."

"How about the building over there?" The first girl pointed to a tenement several rooftops away. "Most of them families in that building moved out, so probably no one will hear us."

They headed in that direction, eager to be out of the hot sun.

"I hope the entrance ain't locked," said the third girl.

They climbed the last dividing wall and went straight to the entrance, which jutted out of the rooftop at a slant. The third girl pulled at the large metal door; it wouldn't budge.

"It's locked," she said to her companions.

41

"Try it the other way," said the first girl. "Let's push in."

They pushed the door, and it opened slightly.

All three girls pushed with all their might, and slowly the door began to open.

"A little more and one of us can slide in and see what's making it get stuck," said the third girl.

The door opened about one and a half feet.

"Good. Let's go in and see what's making it stuck." The first girl slipped through. "Ouch," she said. "There's a man sleeping, I think." She quickly came back out.

"Well?" the second girl asked.

"Wanna come in and see him?" the first girl replied. "It's dark in there. But it was a man; and he was sleeping real sound. He didn't make no noise when I stepped on him."

"Let's go on in and see," said the third girl.

"What if he should wake up?" asked the second girl.

"We'll run real fast," said the first girl.

"Yeah," said the second girl. "Down the stairs. Otherwise he might catch us on the roof. What do you say? O.K.?"

They agreed and slipped in through the partially opened door. They entered the dark hallway carefully, avoiding the body that lay on the floor between the door and the wall.

"See?" The first girl pointed. "He must be fast asleep."

They concentrated as they stared at the body, trying to make things out. After a while, their eyes adjusted to the dark and he became more visible.

"Oh, look! He's got a jacket, and it's from that club," said the third girl.

He lay curled up, facing the wall; they could see his back

clearly. He wore a bright orange jacket. A large picture of the head of a leopard baring its teeth was decaled across the back. Underneath, the words PUERTO RICAN LEOPARDS were stenciled in black.

"It's one of them guys," said the first girl. "You know?" she continued. "He's not moving. Maybe . . . maybe he's dead!"

The girls rushed away from him, going down a few steps into the stairwell.

"What do you think we should do?" asked the second girl.

"Maybe we should find out who he is," the first girl responded.

"He might wake up if we get too near," said the second girl.

They looked at one another and then at the young man. He had not moved and still faced the wall, his body curled up.

"Who's gonna look and see who he is?" asked the first girl.

"Not me."

"Not me."

"Not me neither, then."

They stood silently for a while, and finally the third girl said, "We should go and tell the super of the building."

"That's right. Good idea!"

"I say we should still know who it is," said the first girl. "Let's find out—come on!" She went up the steps.

"Wait," called the second girl. "Be careful; he might wake up."

She stopped and nodded in response, then quickly

43

stepped up to the young man. Leaning over, she looked at his face and ran back to her friends.

"Well, who is it?" they asked.

"It's their leader. You know, that real tough guy. Frankie-Chino!"

"No kidding, him?"

"Wow."

"Yes. And you know," said the first girl, "his eyes are closed . . . and he's not breathing!"

"Really?"

"Honest?"

"Go see for yourself," she told her friends.

"I'm scared he might wake up," said the second girl.

"He won't. He's not breathing," said the first girl.

Holding hands, they went up to him and quickly bent over, looking into his face. They ran back down, a little less scared than before.

"I think he's dead," the second girl said. The third girl nodded in agreement.

"What should we do?" asked the first girl. "I know," she went on, "let's go tell them about it at their clubhouse. It's down in the basement, right next to the candy store on Wales Avenue, off Westchester."

They all looked at each other and shrugged their shoulders.

"Let's do it," said the first girl. "Come on."

"All right."

"Sure."

All three ran down the stairs and out into the street. They hurried, talking in short, anxious sentences, planning how they would tell their story.

"They are real tough guys. Wow, my mother better not find out we went there," said the second girl.

"Oh, we won't tell nobody. It's our secret. Right?"

"Also, we have to promise that we won't let nobody else know . . . about him. Except the Puerto Rican Leopards, of course."

They all promised.

They reached Wales Avenue and went down the old tenement steps leading to the basement clubhouse of the Puerto Rican Leopards. They got to the door and knocked; no one answered. They knocked again and again, waiting for a response. After a while, the first girl tried the door-knob; the lock released, and the door opened.

They walked in slowly, entering a large unkempt room that was damp and dark. A studio couch with large holes, where the stuffing spilled out, was against the center wall. Several old rusted metal kitchen chairs were scattered about the room, some overturned. A broken radio was set on two wooden crates. The center of the cement floor was covered by a large piece of broken and peeling linoleum. Dirty paper cups and plates were strewn about. The room looked dusty and neglected.

"Nobody's here," said the second girl.

"It looks deserted," said the third girl.

"Let's get out of here," said the first girl. All three walked out of the dark basement and out into the street. The afternoon sun shone brightly; it was hot and humid.

"Whew," said the first girl, "it was so much more cooler down there."

Slowly, they walked along tossing the ball to one another until they got back to their building.

"What do you think?" asked the second girl. "Should we tell somebody what we seen?"

"I think we should just forget it. That guy was probably sleeping and woke up already," said the third girl.

"Yeah. We better not; then they'll ask us what we was doing up on the roof and all," said the first girl.

"Let's have another game of ball," said the second girl.

"Let me go first," said the third girl. "I was last before."

"O.K."

"All right."

Bouncing the ball and throwing her leg over it on every third bounce, she sang,

> Once upon a time
> A baby found a dime.
> The dime turned red,
> And the baby fell down dead!

MR. MENDELSOHN

"Psst . . . psst, Mr. Mendelsohn, wake up. Come on now!" Mrs. Suárez said in a low quiet voice. Mr. Mendelsohn had fallen asleep again, on the large armchair in the living room. He grasped the brown shiny wooden cane and leaned forward, his chin on his chest. The small black skull-cap that was usually placed neatly on the back of his head had tilted to one side, covering his right ear. "Come on now. It's late, and time to go home." She tapped him on the shoulder and waited for him to wake up. Slowly, he lifted his head, opened his eyes, and blinked.

"What time is it?" he asked.

"It's almost midnight. Caramba! I didn't even know you was still here. When I came to shut off the lights, I saw you was sleeping."

"Oh . . . I'm sorry. O.K., I'm leaving." With short, slow steps he followed Mrs. Suárez over to the front door.

"Go on now," she said, opening the door. "We'll see you tomorrow."

He walked out into the hallway, stepped about three feet to the left, and stood before the door of his apartment. Mrs. Suárez waited, holding her door ajar, while he carefully searched for the right key to each lock. He had to open seven locks in all.

A small fluffy dog standing next to Mrs. Suárez began to whine and bark.

"Shh—sh, Sporty! Stop it!" she said. "You had your walk. Shh."

"O.K.," said Mr. Mendelsohn, finally opening his door. "Good night." Mrs. Suárez smiled and nodded.

"Good night," she whispered, as they both shut their doors simultaneously.

Mr. Mendelsohn knocked on the door and waited; then tried the doorknob. Turning and pushing, he realized the door was locked, and knocked again, this time more forcefully. He heard Sporty barking and footsteps coming toward the door.

"Who's there?" a child's voice asked.

"It's me—Mr. Mendelsohn! Open up, Yvonne." The door opened, and a young girl, age nine, smiled at him.

"Mami! It's el Señor Mr. Mendelsohn again."

"Tell him to come on in, muchacha!" Mrs. Suárez answered.

"My mother says come on in."

He followed Yvonne and the dog, who leaped up, barking and wagging his tail. Mr. Mendelsohn stood at the kitchen entrance and greeted everyone.

"Good morning to you all!" He had just shaved and trimmed his large black mustache. As he smiled broadly, one could see that most of his teeth were missing. His large bald head was partially covered by his small black skullcap. Thick dark grey hair grew in abundance at the lower back

48

of his head, coming around the front above his ears into short sideburns. He wore a clean white shirt, frayed at the cuffs. His worn-out pinstripe trousers were held up by a pair of dark suspenders. Mr. Mendelsohn leaned on his brown shiny cane and carried a small brown paper bag.

"Mr. Mendelsohn, come into the kitchen," said Mrs. Suárez, "and have some coffee with us." She stood by the stove. A boy of eleven, a young man of about seventeen, and a young pregnant woman were seated at the table.

"Sit here," said the boy, vacating a chair. "I'm finished eating." He stood by the entrance with his sister Yvonne, and they both looked at Mr. Mendelsohn and his paper bag with interest.

"Thank you, Georgie," Mr. Mendelsohn said. He sat down and placed the bag on his lap.

The smell of freshly perked coffee and boiled milk permeated the kitchen.

Winking at everyone, the young man asked, "Hey, what you got in that bag you holding onto, huh, Mr. Mendelsohn?" They all looked at each other and at the old man, amused. "Something special, I bet!"

"Well," the old man replied. "I thought your mama would be so kind as to permit me to make myself a little breakfast here today . . . so." He opened the bag, and began to take out its contents. "I got two slices of rye bread, two tea bags. I brought one extra, just in case anybody would care to join me for tea. And a jar of herring in sour cream."

"Sounds delicious!" said the young man, sticking out his tongue and making a face. Yvonne and Georgie burst out laughing.

"Shh . . . sh." Mrs. Suárez shook her head and looked at

49

her children disapprovingly. "Never mind, Julio!" she said to the young man. Turning to Mr. Mendelsohn, she said, "You got the same like you brought last Saturday, eh? You can eat with us anytime. How about some fresh coffee? I just made it. Yes?" Mr. Mendelsohn looked at her, shrugging his shoulders. "Come on, have some," she coaxed.

"O.K.," he replied. "If it's not too much bother."

"No bother," she said, setting out a place for the old man. "You gonna have some nice fresh bread with a little butter —it will go good with your herring." Mrs. Suárez cut a generous slice of freshly baked bread with a golden crust and buttered it. "Go on, eat. There's a plate and everything for your food. Go on, eat. . . ."

"Would anyone care for some?" Mr. Mendelsohn asked. "Perhaps a tea bag for a cup of tea?"

"No . . . no thank you, Mr. Mendelsohn," Mrs. Suárez answered. "Everybody here already ate. You go ahead and eat. You look too skinny; you better eat. Go on, eat your bread."

The old man began to eat vigorously.

"Can I ask you a question?" Julio asked the old man. "Man, I don't get you. You got a whole apartment next door all to yourself—six rooms! And you gotta come here to eat in this crowded kitchen. Why?"

"First of all, today is Saturday, and I thought I could bring in my food and your mama could turn on the stove for me. You know, in my religion you can't light a fire on Saturday."

"You come here anytime; I turn on the stove for you, don't worry," Mrs. Suárez said.

50

"Man, what about other days? We been living here for about six months, right?" Julio persisted. "And you do more cooking here than in your own place."

"It doesn't pay to turn on the gas for such a little bit of cooking. So I told the gas company to turn it off . . . for good! I got no more gas now, only an electric hot plate," the old man said.

Julio shook his head and sighed. "I don't know—"

"Julio, chico!" snapped Mrs. Suárez, interrupting him, "Basta—it doesn't bother nobody." She looked severely at her son and shook her head. "You gotta go with your sister to the clinic today, so you better get ready now. You too, Marta."

"O.K., Mama," she answered, "but I wanted to see if I got mail from Ralphy today."

"You don't got time. I'll save you the mail; you read it when you get back. You and Julio better get ready; go on." Reluctantly, Marta stood up and yawned, stretching and arching her back.

"Marta," Mr. Mendelsohn said, "you taking care? . . . You know, this is a very delicate time for you."

"I am, Mr. Mendelsohn. Thank you."

"I raised six sisters," the old man said. "I ought to know. Six . . . and married them off to fine husbands. Believe me, I've done my share in life." Yvonne and Georgie giggled and poked each other.

"He's gonna make one of his speeches," they whispered.

". . . I never had children. No time to get married. My father died when I was eleven. I went to work supporting my mother and six younger sisters. I took care of them, and

51

today they are all married, with families. They always call and want me to visit them. I'm too busy and I have no time. . . ."

"Too busy eating in our kitchen," whispered Julio. Marta, Georgie and Yvonne tried not to laugh out loud. Mrs. Suárez reached over and with a wooden ladle managed a light but firm blow on Julio's head.

". . . Only on the holidays, I make some time to see them. But otherwise, I cannot be bothered with all that visiting." Mr. Mendelsohn stopped speaking and began to eat again.

"Go on, Marta and Julio, you will be late for the clinic," Mrs. Suárez said. "And you two? What are you doing there smiling like two monkeys? Go find something to do!"

Quickly, Georgie and Yvonne ran down the hallway, and Julio and Marta left the kitchen.

Mrs. Suárez sat down beside the old man.

"Another piece of bread?" she asked.

"No, thank you very much. . . . I'm full. But it was delicious."

"You too skinny—you don't eat right, I bet." Mrs. Suárez shook her head. "Come tomorrow and have Sunday supper with us."

"I really couldn't."

"Sure, you could. I always make a big supper and there is plenty. All right? Mr. Suárez and I will be happy to have you."

"Are you sure it will be no bother?"

"What are you talking for the bother all the time? One more person is no bother. You come tomorrow. Yes?"

The old man smiled broadly and nodded. This was the

first time he had been invited to Sunday supper with the family.

Mrs. Suárez stood and began clearing away the dishes. "O.K., you go inside; listen to the radio or talk to the kids or something. I got work to do."

Mr. Mendelsohn closed his jar of herring and put it back into the bag. "Can I leave this here till I go?"

"Leave it; I put it in the refrigerator for you."

Leaning on his cane, Mr. Mendelsohn stood up and walked out of the kitchen and down the long hallway into the living room. It was empty. He went over to a large armchair by the window. The sun shone through the window, covering the entire armchair and Mr. Mendelsohn. A canary cage was also by the window, and two tiny yellow birds chirped and hopped back and forth energetically. Mr. Mendelsohn felt drowsy; he shut his eyes. So many aches and pains, he thought. It was hard to sleep at night, but here, well . . . the birds began to chirp in unison and the old man opened one eye, glancing at them, and smiled. Then he shut his eyes once more and fell fast asleep.

When Mr. Mendelsohn opened his eyes, Georgie and Yvonne were in the living room. Yvonne held a deck of playing cards and Georgie read a comic book. She looked at the old man and, holding up the deck of cards, asked, "Do you wanna play a game of War? Huh, Mr. Mendelsohn?"

"I don't know how to play that," he answered.

"It's real easy. I'll show you. Come on . . . please!"

"Well," he shrugged, "sure, why not? Maybe I'll learn something."

Yvonne took a small maple end table and a wooden

53

chair, and set them next to Mr. Mendelsohn. "Now . . ." she began, "I'll shuffle the cards and you cut, and then I throw down a card and you throw down a card and the one with the highest card wins. O.K.? And then, the one with the most cards of all wins the game. O.K.?"

"That's all?" he asked.

"That's all. Ready?" she asked, and sat down. They began to play cards.

"You know, my sister Jennie used to be a great card player," said Mr. Mendelsohn.

"Does she still play?" asked Yvonne.

"Oh . . ." Mr. Mendelsohn laughed. "I don't know any more. She's already married and has kids. She was the youngest in my family—like you."

"Did she go to P.S. 39? On Longwood Avenue?"

"I'm sure she did. All my sisters went to school around here."

"Wow! You must be living here a long time, Mr. Mendelsohn."

"Forty-five years!" said the old man.

"Wowee!" Yvonne whistled. "Georgie, did you hear? Mr. Mendelsohn been living here for forty-five whole years!"

Georgie put down his comic book and looked up.

"Really?" he asked, impressed.

"Yes, forty-five years this summer we moved here. But in those days things were different, not like today. No sir! The Bronx has changed. Then, it was the country. That's right! Why, look out the window. You see the elevated trains on Westchester Avenue? Well, there were no trains then. That was once a dirt road. They used to bring cows through there."

"Oh, man!" Georgie and Yvonne both gasped.

"Sure. These buildings were among the first apartment houses to go up. Four stories high, and that used to be a big accomplishment in them days. All that was here was mostly little houses, like you still see here and there. Small farms, woodlands . . . like that."

"Did you see any Indians?" asked Georgie.

"What do you mean, Indians?" laughed the old man. "I'm not that old, and this here was not the Wild West." Mr. Mendelsohn saw that the children were disappointed. He added quickly, "But we did have carriages with horses. No cars and lots of horses."

"That's what Mami says they have in Puerto Rico—not like here in El Bronx," said Yvonne.

"Yeah," Georgie agreed. "Papi says he rode a horse when he was a little kid in Puerto Rico. They had goats and pigs and all them things. Man, was he lucky."

"Lucky?" Mr. Mendelsohn shook his head. "You—you are the lucky one today! You got school and a good home and clothes. You don't have to go out to work and support a family like your papa and I had to do, and miss an education. You can learn and be somebody someday."

"Someday," said Yvonne, "we are gonna get a house with a yard and all. Mami says that when Ralphy gets discharged from the Army, he'll get a loan from the government and we can pay to buy a house. You know, instead of rent."

Mrs. Suárez walked into the living room with her coat on, carrying a shopping bag.

"Yvonne, take the dog out for a walk, and Georgie come on! We have to go shopping. Get your jacket."

55

Mr. Mendelsohn started to rise. "No," she said, "stay . . . sit down. It's O.K. You can stay and rest if you want."

"All right, Mrs. Suárez," Mr. Mendelsohn said.

"Now don't forget tomorrow for Sunday supper, and take a nap if you like."

Mr. Mendelsohn heard the front door slam shut, and the apartment was silent. The warmth of the bright sun made him drowsy once more. It was so nice here, he thought, a house full of people and kids—like it used to be. He recalled his sisters and his parents . . . the holidays . . . the arguments . . . the laughing. It was so empty next door. He would have to look for a smaller apartment, near Jennie, someday. But not now. Now, it was just nice to sleep and rest right here. He heard the tiny birds chirping and quietly drifted into a deep sleep.

Mr. Mendelsohn rang the bell, then opened the door. He could smell the familiar cooking odors of Sunday supper. For two years he had spent every Sunday at his neighbors'. Sporty greeted him, jumping affectionately and barking.

"Shh—sh . . . down. Good boy," he said, and walked along the hallway toward the kitchen. The room was crowded with people and the stove was loaded with large pots of food, steaming and puffing. Mrs. Suárez was busy basting a large roast. Looking up, she saw Mr. Mendelsohn.

"Come in," she said, "and sit down." Motioning to Julio, who was seated, she continued, "Julio, you are finished, get up and give Mr. Mendelsohn a seat." Julio stood up.

"Here's the sponge cake," Mr. Mendelsohn said, and handed the cake box he carried to Julio, who put it in the refrigerator.

"That's nice. . . . Thank you," said Mrs. Suárez, and placed a cup of freshly made coffee before the old man.

"Would anyone like some coffee?" Mr. Mendelsohn asked. Yvonne and Georgie giggled, looked at one another, and shook their heads.

"You always say that!" said Yvonne.

"One of these days," said Ralphy, "I'm gonna say, 'Yes, give me your coffee,' and you won't have none to drink." The children laughed loudly.

"Don't tease him," Mrs. Suárez said, half smiling. "Let him have his coffee."

"He is just being polite, children," Mr. Suárez said, and shifting his chair closer to Mr. Mendelsohn, he asked, "So . . . Mr. Mendelsohn, how you been? What's new? You O.K.?"

"So-so, Mr. Suárez. You know, aches and pains when you get old. But there's nothing you can do, so you gotta make the best of it."

Mr. Suárez nodded sympathetically, and they continued to talk. Mr. Mendelsohn saw the family every day, except for Mr. Suárez and Ralphy, who both worked a night shift.

Marta appeared in the entrance, holding a small child by the hand.

"There he is, Tato," she said to the child, and pointed to Mr. Mendelsohn.

"Oh, my big boy! He knows, he knows he's my best friend," Mr. Mendelsohn said, and held the brown shiny cane out toward Tato. The small boy grabbed the cane and, shrieking with delight, walked toward Mr. Mendelsohn.

"Look at that, will you?" said Ralphy. "He knows Mr. Mendelsohn better than me, his own father."

"That's because they are always together," smiled Marta. "Tato is learning to walk with his cane!"

Everyone laughed as they watched Tato climbing the old man's knee. Bending over, Mr. Mendelsohn pulled Tato onto his lap.

"Oh . . . he's getting heavy," said Mrs. Suárez. "Be careful."

"Never mind," Mr. Mendelsohn responded, hugging Tato. "That's my best boy. And look how swell he walks, and he's not even nineteen months."

"What a team," Julio said. "Tato already walks like Mr. Mendelsohn and pretty soon he's gonna complain like him, too. . . ." Julio continued to tease the old man, who responded good-naturedly, as everyone laughed.

After coffee, Mr. Mendelsohn sat on the large armchair in the living room, waiting for supper to be ready. He watched with delight as Tato walked back and forth with the cane. Mr. Mendelsohn held Tato's blanket, stuffed bear, and picture book.

"Tato," he called out, "come here. Let me read you a book—come on. I'm going to read you a nice story."

Tato climbed onto the chair and into Mr. Mendelsohn's lap. He sucked his thumb and waited. Mr. Mendelsohn opened the picture book.

"O.K. Now . . ." He pointed to the picture. "A is for Alligators. See that? Look at that big mouth and all them teeth. . . ." Tato yawned, nestled back, and closed his eyes. The old man read a few more pages and shut the book.

The soft breathing and sucking sound that Tato made assured Mr. Mendelsohn that the child was asleep. Such a smart kid. What a great boy, he said to himself. Mr. Mendelsohn was vaguely aware of a radio program, voices, and the small dog barking now and then, just before he too fell into a deep sleep.

This Sunday was very much like all the others; coffee first, then he and Tato would play a bit before napping in the large armchair. It had become a way of life for the old man. Only the High Holy Days and an occasional invitation to a family event, such as a marriage or funeral and so on, would prevent the old man from spending Sunday next door.

It had all been so effortless. No one ever asked him to leave, except late at night when he napped too long. On Saturdays, he tried to observe the Sabbath and brought in his meal. They lit the stove for him.

Mrs. Suárez was always feeding him, just like Mama. She also worried about me not eating, the old man had said to himself, pleased. At first, he had been cautious and had wondered about the food and the people that he was becoming so involved with. That first Sunday, the old man had looked suspiciously at the food they served him.

"What is it?" he had asked. Yvonne and Georgie had started giggling, and had looked at one another. Mrs. Suárez had responded quickly and with anger, cautioning her children; speaking to them in Spanish.

"Eat your food, Mr. Mendelsohn. You too skinny," she had told him.

"What kind of meat is it?" Mr. Mendelsohn insisted.

"It's good for you, that's what it is," Mrs. Suárez answered.

"But I—" Mr. Mendelsohn started.

"Never mind—it's good for you. I prepare everything fresh. Go ahead and eat it," Mrs. Suárez had interrupted. There was a silence as Mr. Mendelsohn sat still, not eating.

"You know, I'm not allowed to eat certain things. In my religion we have dietary laws. This is not—pork or something like it, is it?"

"It's just . . . chicken. Chicken! That's what it is. It's delicious . . . and good for you," she had said with conviction.

"It doesn't look like chicken to me."

"That's because you never ate no chicken like this before. This here is—is called Puerto Rican chicken. I prepare it special. So you gonna eat it. You too skinny."

Mr. Mendelsohn had tried to protest, but Mrs. Suárez insisted. "Never mind. Now I prepare everything clean and nice. You eat the chicken; you gonna like it. Go on!"

And that was all.

Mr. Mendelsohn ate his Sunday supper from then on without doubt or hesitation, accepting the affection and concern that Mrs. Suárez provided with each plateful.

That night in his own apartment, Mr. Mendelsohn felt uneasy. He remembered that during supper, Ralphy had mentioned that his G.I. loan had come through. They would be looking for a house soon, everyone agreed. Not in the Bronx; farther out, near Yonkers: It was more like the country there.

The old man tossed and turned in his bed. That's still a long way off. First, they have to find the house and everything. You don't move just like that! he said to himself. It's

60

gonna take a while, he reasoned, putting such thoughts out of his mind.

Mr. Mendelsohn looked at his new quarters.

"I told you, didn't I? See how nice this is?" his sister Jennie said. She put down the large sack of groceries on the small table.

It was a fair-sized room with a single bed, a bureau, a wooden wardrobe closet, a table, and two chairs. A hot plate was set on a small white refrigerator, and a white metal kitchen cabinet was placed alongside.

"We'll bring you whatever else you need, Louis," Jennie went on. "You'll love it here, I'm sure. There are people your own age, interested in the same things. Here—let's get started. We'll put your things away and you can get nicely settled."

Mr. Mendelsohn walked over to the window and looked out. He saw a wide avenue with cars, taxis and buses speeding by. "It's gonna take me two buses, at least, to get back to the old neighborhood," he said.

"Why do you have to go back there?" Jennie asked quickly. "There is nobody there any more, Louis. Everybody moved!"

"There's shul. . . ."

"There's shul right here. Next door you have a large temple. Twice you were robbed over there. It's a miracle you weren't hurt! Louis, there is no reason for you to go back. There is nothing over there, nothing," Jennie said.

"The trouble all started with that rooming house next door. Those people took in all kinds. . . ." He shook his head. "When the Suárez family lived there we had no problems. But nobody would talk to the landlord about those new people—only me. Nobody cared."

"That's all finished," Jennie said, looking at her watch. "Now look how nice it is here. Come on, let's get started." She began to put the groceries away in the refrigerator and cabinet.

"Leave it, Jennie," he interrupted. "Go on. . . . I'll take care of it. You go on home. You are in a hurry."

"I'm only trying to help," Jennie responded.

"I know, I know. But I lived in one place for almost fifty years. So don't hurry me." He looked around the room. "And I ain't going nowhere now. . . ."

Shaking her head, Jennie said, "Look—this weekend we have a wedding, but next weekend Sara and I will come to see you. I'll call the hotel on the phone first, and they'll let you know. All right?"

"Sure." He nodded.

"That'll be good, Louis. This way you will get a chance to get settled and get acquainted with some of the other residents." Jennie kissed Mr. Mendelsohn affectionately. The old man nodded and turned away. In a moment, he heard the door open and shut.

Slowly, he walked to the sack of groceries and finished putting them away. Then, with much effort, he lifted a large suitcase onto the bed. He took out several photographs. Then he set the photographs upright, arranging them carefully on the bureau. He had pictures of his parents' wedding and of his sisters and their families. There was a photograph of his mother taken just before she died, and another one of Tato.

That picture was taken when he was about two years old,

the old man said to himself. Yes, that's right, on his birthday. . . . There was a party. And Tato was already talking. Such a smart kid, he thought, smiling. Last? Last when? he wondered. Time was going fast for him. He shrugged. He could hardly remember what year it was lately. Just before they moved! He remembered. That's right, they gave him the photograph of Tato. They had a nice house around Gunhill Road someplace, and they had taken him there once. He recalled how exhausted he had been after the long trip. No one had a car, and they had had to take a train and buses. Anyway, he was glad he remembered. Now he could let them know he had moved, and tell them all about what happened to the old neighborhood. That's right, they had a telephone now. Yes, he said to himself, let me finish here, then I'll go call them. He continued to put the rest of his belongings away.

Mr. Mendelsohn sat in the lobby holding on to his cane and a cake box. He had told the nurse at the desk that his friends were coming to pick him up this Sunday. He looked eagerly toward the revolving doors. After a short while, he saw Ralphy, Julio, and Georgie walk through into the lobby.

"Deliveries are made in the rear of the building," he heard the nurse at the desk say as they walked toward him.

"These are my friends, Mrs. Read," Mr. Mendelsohn said, standing. "They are here to take me out."

"Oh, well," said the nurse. "All right; I didn't realize. Here he is then. He's been talking about nothing else but this visit." Mrs. Read smiled.

Ralphy nodded, then spoke to Georgie. "Get Mr. Mendelsohn's overcoat."

63

Quickly, Mr. Mendelsohn put on his coat, and all four left the lobby.

"Take good care of him now . . ." they heard Mrs. Read calling. "You be a good boy now, Mr. Mendelsohn."

Outside, Mr. Mendelsohn looked at the young men and smiled.

"How's everyone?" he asked.

"Good," Julio said. "Look, that's my pickup truck from work. They let me use it sometimes when I'm off."

"That's a beautiful truck. How's everyone? Tato? How is my best friend? And Yvonne? Does she like school? And your Mama and Papa? . . . Marta? . . ."

"Fine, fine. Everybody is doing great. Wait till you see them. We'll be there in a little while," said Julio. "With this truck, we'll get there in no time."

Mr. Mendelsohn sat in the kitchen and watched as Mrs. Suárez packed food into a shopping bag. Today had been a good day for the old man; he had napped in the old armchair and spent time with the children. Yvonne was so grown up, he almost had not recognized her. When Tato remembered him, Mr. Mendelsohn had been especially pleased. Shyly, he had shaken hands with the old man. Then he had taken him into his room to show Mr. Mendelsohn all his toys.

"Now I packed a whole lotta stuff in this shopping bag for you. You gotta eat it. Eat some of my Puerto Rican chicken—it's good for you. You too skinny. You got enough for tomorrow and for another day. You put it in the refrigerator. Also I put some rice and other things."

He smiled as she spoke, enjoying the attention he received.

"Julio is gonna drive you back before it gets too late," she said. "And we gonna pick you up again and bring you back to eat with us. I bet you don't eat right." She shook her head. "O.K.?"

"You shouldn't go through so much bother," he protested mildly.

"Again with the bother? You stop that! We gonna see you soon. You take care of yourself and eat. Eat! You must nourish yourself, especially in such cold weather."

Mr. Mendelsohn and Mrs. Suárez walked out into the living room. The family exchanged good-byes with the old man. Tato, feeling less shy, kissed Mr. Mendelsohn on the cheek.

Just before leaving, Mr. Mendelsohn embraced Mrs. Suárez for a long time, as everybody watched silently.

"Thank you," he whispered.

"Thank you? For what?" Mrs. Suárez said. "You come back soon and have Sunday supper with us. Yes?" Mr. Mendelsohn nodded and smiled.

It was dark and cold out. He walked with effort. Julio carried the shopping bag. Slowly, he got into the pickup truck. The ride back was bumpy and uncomfortable for Mr. Mendelsohn. The cold wind cut right through into the truck, and the old man was aware of the long winter ahead.

His eyelids were so heavy he could hardly open them. Nurses scurried about busily. Mr. Mendelsohn heard voices.

"Let's give him another injection. It will help his breathing. Nurse! Nurse! The patient needs . . ."

The voices faded. He remembered he had gone to sleep after supper last—last when? How many days have I been here . . . here in the hospital? Yes, he thought, now I know where I am. A heart attack, the doctor had said, and then he had felt even worse. Didn't matter; I'm too tired. He heard voices once more, and again he barely opened his eyes. A tall thin man dressed in white spoke to him.

"Mr. Mendelsohn, can you hear me? How do you feel now? More comfortable? We called your family. I spoke to your sister, Mrs. Wiletsky. They should be here very soon. You feeling sleepy? Good. . . . Take a little nap—go on. We'll wake you when they get here, don't worry. Go on now. . . ."

He closed his eyes, thinking of Jennie. She'll be here soon with Esther and Rosalie and Sara. All of them. He smiled. He was so tired. His bed was by the window and a bright warm sash of sunshine covered him almost completely. Nice and warm, he thought, and felt comfortable. The pain had lessened, practically disappeared. Mr. Mendelsohn heard the birds chirping and Sporty barking. That's all right, Mrs. Suárez would let him sleep. She wouldn't wake him up, he knew that. It looked like a good warm day; he planned to take Tato out for a walk later. That's some smart kid, he thought. Right now he was going to rest.

"This will be the last of it, Sara."

"Just a few more things, Jennie, and we'll be out of here."

The two women spoke as they packed away all the items in the room. They opened drawers and cabinets, putting

66

things away in boxes and suitcases.

"What about these pictures on the bureau?" asked Sara.

Jennie walked over and they both looked at the photographs.

"There's Mama and Papa's wedding picture. Look, there's you, Sara, when Jonathan was born. And Esther and . . . look, he's got all the pictures of the entire family." Jennie burst into tears.

"Come on, Jennie; it's all over, honey. He was sick and very old." The older woman comforted the younger one.

Wiping her eyes, Jennie said, "Well, we did the best we could for him, anyway."

"Who is this?" asked Sara, holding up Tato's photo.

"Let me see," said Jennie. "Hummm . . . that must be one of the people in that family that lived next door in the old apartment on Prospect Avenue. You know—remember that Spanish family? He used to visit with them. Their name was . . . Díaz or something like that, I think. I can't remember."

"Oh yes," said Sara. "Louis mentioned them once in a while, yes. They were nice to him. What shall we do with it? Return it?"

"Oh," said Jennie, "that might be rude. What do you think?"

"Well, I don't want it, do you?"

"No." Jennie hesitated. ". . . But let's just put it away. Maybe we ought to tell them what happened. About Louis." Sara shrugged her shoulders. "Maybe I'll write to them," Jennie went on, "if I can find out where they live. They moved. What do you say?"

"I don't care, really." Sara sighed. "I have a lot to do yet. I have to meet Esther at the lawyer's to settle things. And I still have to make supper. So let's get going."

Both women continued to pack, working efficiently and with swiftness. After a while, everything was cleared and put away in boxes and suitcases.

"All done!" said Sara.

"What about this?" asked Jennie, holding up Tato's photograph.

"Do what you want," said Sara. "I'm tired. Let's go."

Looking at the photograph, Jennie slipped it into one of the boxes. "I might just write and let them know."

The two women left the room, closing the door behind them.

THE WRONG LUNCH LINE

Early Spring 1946

The morning dragged on for Yvette and Mildred. They were anxiously waiting for the bell to ring. Last Thursday the school had announced that free Passover lunches would be provided for the Jewish children during this week. Yvette ate the free lunch provided by the school and Mildred brought her lunch from home in a brown paper bag. Because of school rules, free-lunch children and bag-lunch children could not sit in the same section, and the two girls always ate separately. This week, however, they had planned to eat together.

Finally the bell sounded and all the children left the classroom for lunch. As they had already planned, Yvette and Mildred went right up to the line where the Jewish children were filing up for lunch trays. I hope no one asks me nothing, Yvette said to herself. They stood close to each other and held hands. Every once in a while one would squeeze the other's hand in a gesture of reassurance, and they would giggle softly.

The two girls lived just a few houses away from one another. Yvette lived on the top floor of a tenement, in a four-room apartment which she shared with her parents, grand-mother, three older sisters, two younger brothers, and baby sister. Mildred was an only child. She lived with her parents in the three small rooms in back of the candy store they owned.

During this school year, the two girls had become good friends. Every day after public school, Mildred went to a Hebrew school. Yvette went to catechism twice a week, preparing for her First Communion and Confirmation. Most evenings after supper, they played together in front of the candy store. Yvette was a frequent visitor in Mildred's apartment. They listened to their favorite radio programs together. Yvette looked forward to the Hershey's chocolate bar that Mr. Fox, Mildred's father, would give her.

The two girls waited patiently on the lunch line as they slowly moved along toward the food counter. Yvette was delighted when she saw what was placed on the trays: a hard-boiled egg, a bowl of soup that looked like vegetable, a large piece of cracker, milk, and an apple. She stretched over to see what the regular free lunch was, and it was the usual: a bowl of watery stew, two slices of dark bread, milk, and cooked prunes in a thick syrup. She was really glad to be standing with Mildred.

"Hey Yvette!" She heard someone call her name. It was Elba Cruz, one of her classmates. "What's happening? Why are you standing there?"

"I'm having lunch with Mildred today," she answered, and looked at Mildred, who nodded.

"Oh yeah?" Elba said. "Why are they getting a different lunch from us?"

"It's their special holiday and they gotta eat that special food, that's all," Yvette answered.

"But why?" persisted Elba.

"Else it's a sin, that's why. Just like we can't have no meat on Friday," Yvette said.

"A sin. . . . Why—why is it a sin?" This time, she looked at Mildred.

"It's a special lunch for Passover," Mildred said.

"Passover? What is that?" asked Elba.

"It's a Jewish holiday. Like you got Easter, so we have Passover. We can't eat no bread."

"Oh. . . ."

"You better get in your line before the teacher comes," Yvette said quickly.

"You're here!" said Elba.

"I'm only here because Mildred invited me," Yvette answered. Elba shrugged her shoulders and walked away.

"They gonna kick you outta there. . . . I bet you are not supposed to be on that line," she called back to Yvette.

"Dumbbell!" Yvette answered. She turned to Mildred and asked, "Why can't you eat bread, Mildred?"

"We just can't. We are only supposed to eat matzo. What you see there." Mildred pointed to the large cracker on the tray.

"Oh," said Yvette. "Do you have to eat an egg too?"

"No . . . but you can't have no meat, because you can't have meat and milk together . . . like at the same time."

"Why?"

"Because it's against our religion. Besides, it's very bad. It's not supposed to be good for you."

71

"It's not?" asked Yvette.

"No," Mildred said. "You might get sick. You see, you are better off waiting like a few hours until you digest your food, and then you can have meat or the milk. But not together."

"Wow," said Yvette. "You know, I have meat and milk together all the time. I wonder if my mother knows it's not good for you."

By this time the girls were at the counter. Mildred took one tray and Yvette quickly took another.

"I hope no one notices me," Yvette whispered to Mildred. As the two girls walked toward a long lunch table, they heard giggling and Yvette saw Elba and some of the kids she usually ate lunch with pointing and laughing at her. Stupids, thought Yvette, ignoring them and following Mildred. The two girls sat down with the special lunch group.

Yvette whispered to Mildred, "This looks good!" and started to crack the eggshell.

Yvette felt Mildred's elbow digging in her side. "Watch out!" Mildred said.

"What is going on here?" It was the voice of one of the teachers who monitored them during lunch. Yvette looked up and saw the teacher coming toward her.

"You! You there!" the teacher said, pointing to Yvette. "What are you doing over there?" Yvette looked at the woman and was unable to speak.

"What are you doing over there?" she repeated.

"I went to get some lunch," Yvette said softly.

"What? Speak up! I can't hear you."

"I said . . . I went to get some lunch," she said a little louder.

"Are you entitled to a free lunch?"

"Yes."

"Well . . . and are you Jewish?"

Yvette stared at her and she could feel her face getting hot and flushed.

"I asked you a question. Are you Jewish?" Another teacher Yvette knew came over and the lunchroom became quiet. Everyone was looking at Yvette, waiting to hear what was said. She turned to look at Mildred, who looked just as frightened as she felt. Please don't let me cry, thought Yvette.

"What's the trouble?" asked the other teacher.

"This child," the woman pointed to Yvette, "is eating lunch here with the Jewish children, and I don't think she's Jewish. She doesn't— I've seen her before; she gets free lunch, all right. But she looks like one of the—" Hesitating, the woman went on, "She looks Spanish."

"I'm sure she's not Jewish," said the other teacher.

"All right now," said the first teacher, "what are you doing here? Are you Spanish?"

"Yes."

"Why did you come over here and get in that line? You went on the wrong lunch line!"

Yvette looked down at the tray in front of her.

"Get up and come with me. Right now!" Getting up, she dared not look around her. She felt her face was going to burn up. Some of the children were laughing; she could hear the suppressed giggles and an occasional "Ooooh." As she started to walk behind the teacher, she heard her say, "Go back and bring that tray." Yvette felt slightly weak at the knees but managed to turn around, and going back to

73

the table, she returned the tray to the counter. A kitchen worker smiled nonchalantly and removed the tray full of food.

"Come on over to Mrs. Ralston's office," the teacher said, and gestured to Yvette that she walk in front of her this time.

Inside the vice-principal's office, Yvette stood, not daring to look at Mrs. Rachel Ralston while she spoke.

"You have no right to take someone else's place." Mrs. Ralston continued to speak in an even-tempered, almost pleasant voice. "This time we'll let it go, but next time we will notify your parents and you won't get off so easily. You have to learn, Yvette, right from wrong. Don't go where you don't belong. . . ."

Yvette left the office and heard the bell. Lunchtime was over.

Yvette and Mildred met after school in the street. It was late in the afternoon. Yvette was returning from the corner grocery with a food package, and Mildred was coming home from Hebrew school.

"How was Hebrew school?" asked Yvette.

"O.K." Mildred smiled and nodded. "Are you coming over tonight to listen to the radio? 'Mr. Keene, Tracer of Lost Persons' is on."

"O.K.," said Yvette. "I gotta bring this up and eat. Then I'll come by."

Yvette finished supper and was given permission to visit her friend.

74

"Boy, that was a good program, wasn't it, Mildred?" Yvette ate her candy with delight.

Mildred nodded and looked at Yvette, not speaking. There was a long moment of silence. They wanted to talk about it, but it was as if this afternoon's incident could not be mentioned. Somehow each girl was afraid of disturbing that feeling of closeness they felt for one another. And yet when their eyes met they looked away with an embarrassed smile.

"I wonder what's on the radio next," Yvette said, breaking the silence.

"Nothing good for another half hour," Mildred answered. Impulsively, she asked quickly, "Yvette, you wanna have some matzo? We got some for the holidays."

"Is that the cracker they gave you this afternoon?"

"Yeah. We can have some."

"All right." Yvette smiled.

Mildred left the room and returned holding a large square cracker. Breaking off a piece, she handed it to Yvette.

"It don't taste like much, does it?" said Yvette.

"Only if you put something good on it," Mildred agreed, smiling.

"Boy, that Mrs. Ralston sure is dumb," Yvette said, giggling. They looked at each other and began to laugh loudly.

"Old dumb Mrs. Ralston," said Mildred, laughing convulsively. "She's scre . . . screwy."

"Yeah," Yvette said, laughing so hard tears began to roll down her cheeks. "Dop . . . dopey . . . M . . . Mi . . . Mrs. Ra . . . Ral . . . ston. . . ."

A LESSON IN FORTUNE-TELLING

Miss Braun was busy writing the morning's assignment on the blackboard. She spoke to the class as she wrote.

"Turn to page forty-eight. All ready? There are twenty sentences. Some are correct, and some are incorrect. Look for the object . . ."

The door opened and Mrs. Gevertz, the vice-principal, stood at the entrance.

"Miss Braun? Sorry to disturb the lesson, but your new pupil is here. The one we spoke about?"

"Oh," said Miss Braun, "yes."

"Well, she's right here, ready to join the class." Mrs. Gevertz walked in, followed by a girl about fourteen years old.

The girl had a bright-orange scarf wrapped around her head and tied securely in the back. Dark bangs and side locks framed her face, which was heavily made up with eye shadow, dark lipstick, and bright rouge spots. She wore large gold earrings, long strands of multicolored beads around her neck, and lots of bracelets. Her short-sleeved purple blouse was cut low at the bodice and fitted snugly over her full breasts. She had on several skirts; the top one was bright green and the underskirts were different lengths and colors. Her bare feet were dirty, and her toenails were painted a dark green.

"Wow . . . it's a gypsy!"

"Look at that. . . ."

"Shh," Miss Braun said, frowning at her class.

"Jasmine," Mrs. Gevertz said, "this is Miss Braun, your new teacher. And this is Class 6A-4, your new class. You will be going to school every day from now on, right here!" Mrs. Gevertz continued with a broad smile. "This is Jasmine Farrakhian."

Jasmine stood with her hands folded, looking at the floor. The teachers stared at each other silently.

"All right now," Mrs. Gevertz said. "Perhaps you could show Jasmine to her seat, Miss Braun."

Miss Braun looked over her class and then pointed to several children in the first half of the middle row.

"Ramona and Mary each move back one seat. Mary, please move back into Gordon's seat—he's out today. I'll reassign him tomorrow."

The children obediently moved back, leaving the very first seat vacant.

"Very well," continued Miss Braun. "Wait . . . wait, come back, Ramona; you sit in the front seat. Leave the second seat for Jasmine, since she is—uh—much taller." Everyone waited, looking at Jasmine.

"Please go over and sit in your seat, Jasmine," Mrs. Gevertz said.

Without looking at anyone, Jasmine swiftly walked over and sat down. The beads and bracelets rattled and clicked as she settled herself in her seat.

"All right. I'll leave you now with your new pupil, and

you can all get acquainted." Mrs. Gevertz quickly exited.

Miss Braun continued with the lesson, stopping every once in a while to silence the whispering and chattering. Finally, the lunch bell rang.

"Very well, class," said Miss Braun, "you are dismissed." They all jumped out of their seats, some grabbing lunch bags, and headed out of the door.

She walked over to Jasmine. "You may come with me. We have some lunch for you in the lunchroom. But today I think you had better eat in the office."

After lunch, the children returned to their classroom discussing their new classmate.

"I know where she lives," said Hannibal. "Right on Longwood Avenue, around the corner from Prospect, in a store. I seen them—there is a whole bunch. They got blankets and sheets and material hanging on the windows so you can't see inside. They all dress like her and they don't got no shoes. Except the men, they wear shoes . . . I think."

"Oh, yeah, I seen them too. Man, they're all over El Bronx," said Joey. "They tell your fortune. They are always calling you in when you walk by there."

"My mother says to be careful not to go inside when they call you," said Ramona. "They lived in my building once, and—"

"You know her?" asked Joey.

"No, not her," replied Ramona. "Another family of gypsies. Anyway, my mother said—"

"Are they still living there?" interrupted Joey.

"No!" Ramona answered, annoyed. "They move a lot;

78

they don't stay in one place long—at least that's what my mother says. Anyway, like I was saying, my mother told me when I was a little kid never to go into their house, because they might steal me—"

"Ha!" Hannibal interrupted. "Who's gonna steal you? You so ugly, that's what made them move, I bet!"

Everyone began to laugh. Ramona made a face at Hannibal.

"See?" he continued, pointing at Ramona. "I told you she was ugly. . . ." Delighted that he had an audience, Hannibal said, "Man, she's jealous because she ain't got no maracas to shake, like Jasmine. Man! What a pair of shakers she got. . . . Not like flat chest."

Ramona turned away and began to look at her workbook, ignoring Hannibal.

The laughing stopped and the children returned to their seats when Miss Braun and Jasmine walked into the room.

The children sat with Jasmine in the lunchroom. She ate the free lunch provided daily by the public school. Jasmine had been attending school for two weeks; everyone was quite used to her by now. She had removed the scarf from her head. She wore a loose-fitting cotton housedress, a pair of silver sandals, and dark mesh stockings.

Most of the group sitting with her were girls, although several boys had begun to sit nearby, anxious to hear what Jasmine had to say. Hannibal and Joey always sat with Jasmine during some part of each lunch hour.

"Read my palm. You promised you would today," said Ramona. "You said Friday, and today is Friday."

"All right . . ." Jasmine said, "if you want me to."

"You promised us a story," some of the others protested. They were all intrigued by the stories she told and the way she could read palms, foretelling the future.

"I did promise Ramona," said Jasmine. "I'll tell you a story on Monday—one about the magicians in India and how they can charm snakes."

"Oh, boy!"

"Tell us now."

"Come on, Jasmine," Ramona pleaded. "You did promise."

Jasmine smiled, looking at everyone gathered about her. "If you don't interrupt, and if you are quiet," she told Ramona, "I'll tell your future. But you must concentrate, or the powers won't work."

"Oh, yes!" Ramona nodded.

"Shh . . . sh," Jasmine went on, and closed her eyes. "I have to concentrate . . . to see if I can get the right vibrations. Shh. Put your right palm, facing up, right here in my hand, Ramona." Quickly, Ramona did as she was told. Jasmine opened her eyes. "Ah . . . ha . . . ummm. Ahhhh . . ." she murmured, gently tracing the lines on Ramona's palm with her fingertips.

"What do you see? What do you see? Huh?" Ramona cried.

"Shh," Jasmine whispered. "Don't disturb the powers. I see . . . umm . . . I see . . . Very interesting. Ah ha! You will travel, yes. It's getting good and clear now. You will travel to faraway lands and meet many interesting people. I see . . . I see. But— Tsk! Tsk!" Jasmine stopped and shook her head.

"What? What's the matter? Tell me, please!" Ramona said, breathless.

"Be calm," Jasmine said, reassuringly. "There is a very tall, fair, handsome stranger waiting for you. But—well . . ."

"Well what? What?"

"You must learn some things first, or you will lose this opportunity to change your life, and all the wonderful adventures that are waiting for you."

"Tell me. . . . Oh, please, Jasmine, please!" Ramona said.

"You, Ramona Pérez, must learn to give more and to trust more, and when you are asked by a friend someday for a great favor, you must not refuse. Or your good qualities will disappear! No one will ever know who Ramona really is, and how kind she can really be." Jasmine paused.

A large group had gathered around Jasmine and Ramona. Some were now standing on benches, trying to hear and see what was going on.

"What is going on here?" A tall woman began to break up the group. "Go on back to your seats, right now! Stop this at once!"

Jasmine dropped Ramona's hand, and both girls turned away from each other.

"Listen," said the woman, speaking to Jasmine, "you stop this hocus-pocus of palm reading, or I'll bring you to the principal myself. Just try it one more time. Do you hear?"

"Yes, Mrs. MacEverly," Jasmine replied, nodding.

The woman turned abruptly and walked away. Jasmine shrugged her shoulders, sticking her tongue out at the woman.

"Are you finished?" Ramona asked.

"Yes," said Jasmine.

"Here," said Ramona, "take this pear. Go on, take it. I saved it for you."

"I don't charge. You don't have to give me anything," replied Jasmine.

"I know. But here . . . I want you to have it."

Smiling, Jasmine took the pear and put it into a paper bag. Every lunch hour she would read palms or tell a story. The children would give her gifts, and although she mildly protested she always accepted whatever was offered. They gave her money, sometimes, as well as food. When she admired some trinket, the owner would give it to her as well.

"What did you mean, that—I must do a favor or I will not get to travel and all?" asked Ramona.

"I only told what I seen," said Jasmine.

"She told me almost the same thing," said Mary. "I understood, so I'm gonna get to travel and everything."

"Maybe Mary understands the powers better than you, Ramona," said Jasmine.

Ramona looked at Mary and Jasmine. "I get it too, don't worry!" she said, annoyed.

"I can only advise what I see," said Jasmine. "I can only tell what is there. I don't know no more than nobody else. I was only born with these powers. They are from God."

The children went on talking among themselves. They listened to Jasmine and compared their futures. They were all destined to travel and meet someone someday. However, each would first have to be tested by a good friend.

The bell rang and the children started to clear their

lunch trays and lunch bags before returning to their class-rooms.

Hannibal and Joey waited for Jasmine, walking back to class with her. They did this every day.

"Hey, when you gonna read our palms, man?" asked Hannibal.

"Yeah, you did promise, and so far you only reading the girls' palms. That's not fair," said Joey.

"I'll read yours, don't worry," said Jasmine. "Why don't you come to where I live tomorrow? You know, on Long-wood Avenue. I'll give you a good reading there."

"Wow, man!" said Joey. "Great, huh, Hannibal?"

"O.K.," Hannibal said. "Thanks. Joey and me, we'll do that."

Another bell sounded and they rushed back to class, hoping to get there before Miss Braun.

"Oh, man. When Jasmine comes in, I'm gonna beat the shit out of her," said Hannibal angrily.

"I'm gonna help," nodded Joey.

The children began filing into the classroom and going to their seats. Hannibal and Joey stood by Miss Braun's desk, looking toward the doorway.

When Miss Braun entered, they both sat in their seats. She began her Monday morning roll call. Miss Braun noted that Jasmine was absent for the first time since she had started school.

Hannibal continued to wait, anxiously looking at the door. The morning passed, then lunch, then dismissal time.

After school, Hannibal, Joey, Ramona, Mary, and Ca-silda all walked toward Longwood and Prospect Avenue.

"I'm no sucketa, man! If I don't get that money back, Papi is gonna skin me alive!" said Hannibal.

"I was lucky," said Joey. "I only had fifty cents."

"I wish you would tell us exactly what happened," said Ramona.

"Yeah. How we gonna help if we don't know the whole story?" said Mary.

"She is some phony . . . and her whole family too! She invited me and Joey, right? Like I told you on Saturday. So we got there and went inside the store. Jasmine was there and told us to come on in the back. We did. And there was a room full of rugs and pillows and material on the floors and walls, and some mattresses too. Anyway, she introduced us to this old lady, all dressed up in them clothes. You know—with a rag tied on her head and every-thing. Man, she was real fat . . . and she smelled."

"She had no teeth," Joey interrupted.

"That's right, man—una fea . . . ugly! Well, she said she is gonna read our palms way better than Jasmine, be-cause she got great powers and can tell our future."

"That's right!" said Joey.

"I show her my palm, and then she asked Joey to show her his palm. She looks, but don't say nothing. Then she asked us how much money we got. Because she will bless our money—that way we will never, ever be broke again, in our whole lives! Well, I say I only got a dollar, although I got another five dollars on me. But that's money Papi gave me to pay Mr. Mendoza at the botánica for the new statue of Santa Barbara. Joey tells her he only got fifty

84

cents. She takes his money and begins to mumble over it, making all kinds of signs with her hands, and then she gives him his money back. Right, Joey?"

"That's right, man!" Joey said. "And she told me my future. . . . Everything's gonna be great and cool and fine!"

"Then comes my turn. I give her my dollar and she mumbles over it again, you know, making all them signs and things. And gives me back my dollar. She tells me my future—everything is real rosy and gorgeous. I feel great, right? But then, after she finishes, she grabs me by my shoulders and says to look into her eyes. I better tell her the truth, she says. She knows I have more money. . . . Because if I don't and she can't bless it, I will spend the rest of my life broke! Man, not one penny! So I felt scared and I gave it to her—what a jerk! I gave her Papi's five-dollar bill." Hannibal stopped speaking and shook his head, looking away as he felt himself flushing with embarrassment.

"Come on, Hannibal, please," the girls urged.

"All right, well," Hannibal continued. "She takes the five dollars and mumbles over them again, you know, the whole business. Then she makes a sound in her throat, like she's choking . . . and opens up her mouth . . . and spits up a big green mess right on the five-dollar bill. It was disgusting!"

"Oooo . . ."

"Ugh—ugh."

"Disgusting."

"Then she holds it out to me all gooey and says she better keep it for me, and sticks it inside her blouse, way down in her fat tits!"

"Ooh," said Mary. "I'm gonna be sick."

"I can't stand it," Casilda said. "I'm gonna throw up!"

"That's right. What could I do?" Hannibal said. "That ugly witch, man . . . and them pair of watermelons."

Joey began to laugh, and everyone started to giggle and scream.

After a while, Hannibal said, "It's not funny. Even if I had the nerve to touch that money, man, she just told us to leave; practically threw us out."

"Where was Jasmine?" asked Ramona.

"Noplace. We didn't see her again," said Hannibal.

"We even waited outside and everything," said Joey. "We even looked for her the whole weekend. But she never came out of the store."

"What am I gonna do? When Papi goes to the botánica, Mr. Mendoza is gonna tell him I never paid the bill," Hannibal said. "I'll be dead—Papi will kill me. I gotta get my money back . . . I gotta. I'm gonna choke it outta her!"

"Don't worry. We'll help you," said Ramona.

"O.K.," said Hannibal. "Don't forget, just ask real nice for her. Say like . . . we got something for Jasmine from the teacher in school, but like it's in one of your houses. Could she please come out for just a minute? And we'll be waiting down the block. Just bring her out. O.K.? Then I'll fix her!" Hannibal made a fist.

They all walked at a fast pace until they got within a few yards of the store.

"We'll wait here in this building, right inside the doorway," said Hannibal.

"I hope we are doing the right thing," said Ramona, looking at her two friends.

86

"Come on," said Joey. "We have to help our boy. Are you with us or not?"

"O.K., all right," said Ramona.

"Don't forget now, be cool," Hannibal called out, as Ramona, Mary, and Casilda walked up to the storefront. Hannibal and Joey watched carefully. The three girls walked in.

A few moments later they returned.

"What happened?" asked Hannibal.

"Nobody is there," said Casilda.

"That's right—they are all gone," said Ramona.

"The place is empty. Come and see," said Mary.

Quickly, Hannibal and Joey followed the girls up to the store. The large windows were bare and the store was empty. The door was unlocked and they walked inside.

"In here is where she took us." Hannibal walked into the back and went into a room on the left. The children looked around. Except for an empty milk container and some old newspapers thrown about, the rooms were completely empty.

"That phony!" Hannibal yelled. "All them reading of palms and all that is just a fakería, and you all believed it, too!"

"I never really believed her," protested Ramona.

"Me neither," said Mary.

"Or me," agreed Casilda.

"What?" cried Hannibal. "What about the time you gave her a nickel? Man, I seen you! And you, too, Mary . . . you gave her your bracelet!"

"Listen," Joey said. "We all believed her. . . . Like she

was telling us things for our own good."

"I wonder why Jasmine done this to you and Joey," said Casilda.

"Hey, listen!" said Mary. "I know: because they forced her to do it. Like if she don't do what they tell her, they'll beat her up!"

"Yeah," agreed Ramona. "Maybe they said you do this . . . or else we'll punish you bad!"

"No," said Hannibal. "No! Because she looked too happy about it when she brought us in to meet that old lady. All smiles. Right, Joey?"

"I guess so." Joey hesitated.

"Man, you was there." Hannibal interrupted. "You know it's true!"

"I know, but she was nice sometimes," answered Joey.

"She was," agreed Mary. "And she sure told some good stories."

"Yeah," said Casilda. "Them mysteries were the best. I used to love those stories."

"Boy," said Hannibal, "she's so nice, huh? How come she just disappeared? You tell me!"

"Anyway," Ramona said, "she always told us the same things about our fortunes, to everybody! We are all gonna travel and meet some handsome guy and be rich. First we gotta listen to a good friend and do what she says."

"I told you she's a phony! That's what she is!" Hannibal shouted. His voice resounded in the empty store. The children looked at him, startled. "Bunch of mierda—all that crap! Now what am I gonna tell Papi?" His voice broke, and he struggled to keep back the tears.

"Let's go talk to the janitor of the building," Joey said quickly. "He'll know what to do, Hannibal. He'll tell us where they moved, and we could tell the police."

"Good idea. Sure," everyone agreed.

Hannibal turned away and they could hear him sobbing quietly. After a few moments, Joey said, "Come on, Hannibal. We'll all talk to the janitor and get some information."

Blinking, Hannibal wiped the tears from his face with his shirt sleeves. "I don't care; them people are always moving. They'll probably be gone before we find out where Jasmine is." He shrugged.

"Let's try anyway," said Ramona.

"Listen," said Casilda, "she might write us a letter telling us what happened, and we'll know where she's living."

"Maybe she didn't move too far and we can find her," said Mary.

They all walked out of the empty store and into the street.

"Here, Hannibal," pointed Joey. "Let's go inside and talk to the janitor."

Wiping his eyes again, Hannibal followed his friends into the building.

UNCLE CLAUDIO

Jaime and Charlie sat on the stoop waiting for the rest of their family to come down. They were all going to the airport to see Uncle Claudio and Aunt Chela take the plane back to Puerto Rico.

Charlie had arrived in the Bronx very early this morning with his parents and older sisters. They had driven in from Manhattan. The two boys were first cousins. They saw each other only on special holidays and at family meetings, and today they were glad to be together again.

It was a warm spring Saturday morning. People were still in their apartments and the streets were empty. The boys sat silently, watching the traffic roll by and listening to the faraway sounds coming from inside the tenements. People were beginning to open their windows and turn on their radios. After a while, Jaime stood up and stretched.

"How about a game of stoop ball, Charlie?" he asked, smiling and holding up a Spalding ball.

"Better not," warned Charlie. "I got my good clothes on. You too, Jaime. We'll get it if we get dirty."

Bouncing the ball quickly against the stoop steps a few times, Jaime stopped and sighed. "You're right," he said.

"They sure are taking their sweet time coming down, ain't they?"

"True," answered Jaime, "but they gotta be at the airport at a certain time, so they can't be too late."

"Jaime, do you know why Uncle Claudio is going back to Puerto Rico so fast?" asked Charlie. "He only been here a few months. My mother and father were just talking this morning about how foolish he is to leave. Giving up a good job and good pay and all."

"My mother and father say the same thing like yours. But I know why he's going back to Puerto Rico."

"You do?"

"Yeah," answered Jaime, "I do."

"Tell me."

"Well, I came home from playing ball one day, I guess about a couple of weeks ago. As I came up the stairs I heard a noise, like someone crying. When I came to my floor, there was Uncle Claudio, standing in front of our door. He had his face buried in his hands and was crying out loud."

"Crying?" interrupted Charlie.

"Yes, he was. Because I tapped him and he turned around. His face was full of tears, and when he saw me he just took out his handkerchief, blew his nose, and went into our apartment real quick."

"Why was he crying?"

"I didn't know why, then. He went right into his room, and I forgot about it. But later that evening, I was doing my homework in my room and I heard a lotta noise coming from the kitchen. It sounded like a big argument so

91

I went to see what was happening. Papi was standing and shouting at Uncle Claudio, and Aunt Chela was crying and wiping her eyes. My mother was trying to calm down my father."

"What were they saying?"

"Well, Papi was telling Uncle Claudio that he was an ungrateful brother to be going back to Humacao, after all he and Mami had done for him and Aunt Chela. You know, get them jobs and all. Well, all of a sudden Uncle Claudio jumped up, clenching his fists at Papi. You know what a bad temper my father has, so I thought, Uh-oh, here it comes; they are gonna stomp each other. But when Papi put up his hands to fight back, Uncle Claudio sat down and began to cry. Burst right out into tears just like in the hallway!" Jaime paused and nodded.

"Wow," said Charlie. "Did he tell why he was crying?"

"Wait, I'm coming to that. At first, everybody started asking him a whole lotta questions. He kept saying in Spanish, 'No puede ser,' something like that, you know, like 'It can't never be.' Like that. Then he started to tell why he can't stay here in this country. First, he says there are too many people all living together with no place to go. In his own home, in Humacao, people take it easy and know how to live. They got respect for each other, and know their place. At home, when he walks down the street, he is Don Claudio. But here, in New York City, he is Don Nobody, that's what he said. He doesn't get no respect here. Then he tells something that happened to him that day, in the subway, that he says made him make up his mind to go back home."

"What was that?"

"Well, he got on at his regular station downtown and there was no seats. So he stands, like always, and he notices two young men whispering to each other and pointing at him. At first he don't recognize them. But then one of them looks familiar. They are both well dressed, with suits and ties. One guy waves to him and smiles, so he waves back. Then the guy starts to call out to him by his first name. He says he is Carlito, the son of a lady called Piedad. She used to work for my father and Uncle Claudio's family back in Puerto Rico. The lady used to do the cleaning and cooking, and she was fired. Uncle Claudio says that this young guy is talking real loud and thanks him for firing his mother, because they came to this country and now are doing real well. He even told Uncle Claudio he has no bad feelings and offered him his seat. Then he asked Uncle Claudio where he worked and offered him a better job in his place. Well, Uncle Claudio said he was so embarrassed he got off before his stop, just to get away from that young guy."

"He did?" asked Charlie. "Why?"

"That's exactly what my Papi asked him. Why? Well, Uncle Claudio got real red in the face and started hollering at Papi. He said that in Humacao the maid's son would never talk to him like that. Here, that punk can wear a suit and tie while he has to wear dirty clothes all day. Back home in Humacao, Uncle Claudio says he could get that guy fired and make him apologize for the way he spoke to him, calling him by his first name like that. His mother was caught stealing food and was fired . . . and that she

93

was lucky they did not put her in jail! Anyway, Papi tries to explain to him that things are different here. That people don't think like that, and that these things are not important. That there are better opportunities here in the future for Uncle Claudio's sons. And that Uncle Claudio has to be patient and learn the new ways here in this country." Jaime stopped talking for a moment.

"What did Uncle Claudio say?"

"He got really mad at Papi," said Jaime. "He says that Papi is losing all his values here in New York, and that he don't want his boys to come here, ever. That he is glad he left them in Humacao. There, they know that their father is somebody. He says he is ashamed of his younger brother—you know, my father. Anyway, everybody tried to calm him down and talk him out of going. Even Aunt Chela. I think she likes it here. But he got so excited he jumped up and made the sign of the cross and swore by Jesucristo and la Virgen María that he will never come back to El Bronx again! That was it, he made up his mind to go back, right there!"

"That was it?"

"Yes," Jaime nodded. "That's what happened."

"I don't know," said Charlie, shaking his head. "But I don't care who I meet on the subway, because I may never meet them again. I never see the same people on the subway twice even. Do you? Maybe Uncle Claudio didn't know that."

"You are right, but it wouldn't make no difference because he just made up his mind to leave."

"Anyway," Charlie said, "what's so bad about what that

94

guy said? In fact I thought he seemed nice—giving him his seat and all. Maybe it was something else, and he's not saying the truth."

"No," Jaime said, "that was it. I know; I was there."

"Well, that's no big deal if you ask me. I thought it was something bad," Charlie said.

"I know," said Jaime, "and when I asked Papi why Uncle Claudio got so excited and has to leave, he said that Uncle Claudio lives in another time and that he is dreaming instead of facing life."

"What does that mean?" asked Charlie.

"I asked him the same thing. I don't know what that means neither. And Papi told me that when I grow up I'll understand. Then he started to laugh a whole lot and said that maybe I'll never understand."

"That's what your father said?"

"That's what he said. Nothing else," answered Jaime.

"Well . . ." Charlie shrugged his shoulders and looked at Jaime.

They sat silently for a while, enjoying the bright sun as it warmed their bodies and the stone steps of the stoop.

Very young children played, some on the sidewalk, others in the street. They chalked areas for different games, forming groups. The men were lining up in front of their parked cars with buckets of water, detergent, car wax, and tool boxes. They called out to one another as they began the long and tedious ritual of washing, polishing and fixing their secondhand automobiles.

Windows opened; some of the women shook out the bedclothes, others leaned against the mattresses placed on the sills for an airing and looked out along the avenue. The streets were no longer empty. People hustled and bustled back and forth, and the avenue vibrated with activity.

Jaime and Charlie grew restless.

"Too bad we can't go over to the schoolyard and play ball," said Jaime.

"Here they come at last!" said Charlie.

Uncle Claudio walked by with his wife, Chela. The boys noticed that he wore the same outfit he had arrived with last year: a white suit, white shirt with a pale-blue tie, white shoes, and a very pale beige, wide-brimmed, panama hat. Aunt Chela had a brand-new dress and hat.

The adults talked among themselves as they decided how to group the families into the two cars.

"We wanna ride together, Papi. Please, me and Charlie!" Jaime pulled his father's arm.

"O.K.," said his father, "you two jump in." He pointed to one of the cars.

Jaime and Charlie sat together, enjoying the ride.

"What do you think? If we get back in time, how about going to the schoolyard and have a game of stickball? You can meet all my friends," said Jaime.

"Right!" answered Charlie.

PRINCESS

"Can I take Princess for a walk later?" Judy asked. "Please, Don Osvaldo?"

"We'll see . . . later," Don Osvaldo said. "Let me finish now with your order." He checked the handwritten list of groceries against the items stacked on the counter. "A quarter pound of salt butter, fifteen cents' worth of fatback, two pounds of dried red beans . . ."

Judy played with Princess as she waited for him to pack the groceries. "Sit . . . sit up, Princess. That's a good girl. Nice. Now shake hands. Give me your paw. Right paw! Left paw! Good. Good." The little dog wagged her tail and licked Judy's hand.

"O.K., Judy, I got everything your Mama ordered here in the bag."

"Thank you, Don Osvaldo; put it on our bill."

"I already did," he said, closing a large thick ledger. The grey binding on the ledger was worn, frayed, and filthy with grease spots from constant use. Don Osvaldo would jot down whatever his credit customers bought, including how much it cost. Every name was there in the book, in alphabetical order; a clear record for all to see. At the end of each month, before any more credit was extended, customers were obliged to settle accounts according to the ledger.

"Can I come back and take Princess for a walk?" Judy asked again.

"All right," he said.

"I'm coming back to take you for a walk later," she said to the little dog, and patted her on the head.

Princess began to whine and bark after Judy. Don Osvaldo looked at the dog and smiled. "Nereida, Nereida," he called into the back of the store.

"What is it?" his wife asked.

"Princess is crying—she wants to go with Judy for a walk."

"She's too smart for her own good," his wife said, coming into the store. "Give her something to make her feel better. . . . Go on."

Don Osvaldo went over to the meat counter and removed a hunk of boiled ham. Taking a sharp knife, he cut off a small piece and fed it to the dog. Amused, they watched Princess as she chewed the piece of ham, then sat up begging for more.

"She's so clever," said Doña Nereida, and patted the dog affectionately.

Five years ago a customer had given them the white fluffy-haired puppy, which Doña Nereida had decided to call Princess. Princess was loving and friendly, and showed her gratitude by being obedient. Osvaldo and Nereida Negrón lavished all their affection on the little dog and doted on her. They had no children, hobbies, or interests other than their store, Bodega Borinquén, a grocery specializing in tropical foods, which they kept open seven days a week;

and Princess. The dog shared the small sparsely furnished living quarters in the back of the store with her owners. There, she had her own bed and some toys to play with. Doña Nereida knitted sweaters for Princess and shopped for the fanciest collars and leashes she could find. A child's wardrobe unit had been purchased especially for her.

Customers would comment among themselves:

"That dog eats steak and they only eat tuna fish."

"Princess has better furniture than they have."

"I wish my kids ate as well as that mutt. It's not right, you know. God cannot justify this." And so on.

Despite all the gossip and complaints about the dog, no one dared say anything openly to Don Osvaldo or Doña Nereida.

Customers had to agree that Princess herself was a friendly little animal, and pleasant to look at. When children came into the store to shop they would pet her, and she was gentle with them, accepting their attention joyfully.

Princess was especially fond of Judy, who frequently took her out and taught her tricks. At first, Don Osvaldo and Doña Nereida were worried about letting Judy take Princess for walks. "Hold on to that leash. You mustn't let her get near other dogs; especially those male dogs," they warned. But several months had gone by and Judy and the dog always returned safe and sound. Actually, neither owner liked to leave the store, and they were silently grateful that Judy could take Princess out for some air.

"Mami, can I go back downstairs and take Princess for a walk?" Judy asked her mother.

Her mother had emptied the brown grocery bag and was checking the items.

"Look at that! Fifteen cents' worth of fatback and look at the tiny piece he sends. Bendito!" She shook her head. "I have to watch that man, and she's no better. Didn't I tell you to check anything that he has to weigh?" Judy looked at her mother, expecting her to complain as always about Don Osvaldo and Doña Nereida. "Because we have to buy on credit, they think they can cheat us. When I have cash I will not buy there. I cannot trust them. They charge much more than any other store, but they can get away with it because we buy on credit. I would like to see him charge a cash-paying customer what he does me!"

"Mami, can I go to walk Princess now?" Judy asked again.

"Why do you want to walk that dog? You are always walking that dog. What are you, their servant girl, to walk that stupid dog?"

"I'm the one who wants to walk her. . . . I love Princess. Please may I—"

"Go on!" her mother interrupted, waving her hands in a gesture of annoyance.

Before her mother could change her mind, Judy quickly left the apartment. Her little brother, Angel, had had another asthma attack today, and she knew her mother was in a lousy mood. After her father's death, Judy had moved into this neighborhood with her family: her mother, older sister Blanca, older brother William, and little brother Angel. That was three years ago, when she was just eight. The family had been on public assistance since almost immediately after her father had died. Her mother was always worried about making ends meet, but she was especially hard to live with whenever Angel got sick.

She ran toward the grocery store, anxious to take Princess for her walk. Judy had wanted to have a pet ever since she could remember. It was the one thing that she had always prayed for at Christmas and on her birthday, but her mother absolutely refused. Once she had brought home a stray cat and her little brother Angel had had a severe asthma attack. After that, she was positive that she could never ever have a pet. No matter how she had reasoned, her mother could not be persuaded to change her mind.

"I could give the cat my food, Mami. You don't have to spend no money. And during the day I could find a place to keep it until I got home from school."

"No. We cannot make ends meet to feed human beings, and I am not going to worry about animals. Besides, there's Angel and his allergies." Her mother always won out.

If Papi had lived, maybe things could be different, Judy often thought. But since she could play with Princess and take her out, that was almost like having her own dog, and she had learned to be content with that much.

When Judy arrived at the store Doña Nereida had Princess all ready.

"See, Judy," Doña Nereida said, "she's got a new leash —pale-blue with tiny silver studs. She looks good in blue, don't you think so?" she asked. "It goes with her coloring. Her fur is so nice and white."

The little dog ran, tugging at the leash, and Judy followed, laughing.

Outside in the street, Judy shouted, "Ready, get set . . .

101

go!" Quickly, Judy and Princess began to run, as usual, in the direction of the schoolyard. Once they got there, Judy unleashed Princess and she ran freely, chasing her and some of the other children.

They were all used to Princess, and would pet her, run with her, and sometimes even play a game of ball with the little dog. They watched as Princess followed Judy's commands: She could sit up, roll over, play dead, retrieve, and shake hands. Everyone at the schoolyard treated Princess as if she belonged to Judy and asked her permission first before they played or ran with the little dog. And Princess behaved as if she were Judy's dog. She listened and came obediently when Judy called her. After they had finished playing, Judy leashed Princess and they walked back to the store.

"Did you have a good time?" Doña Nereida asked when they returned. "Come inside with Mama. . . . She has a little something for you," she said to Princess.

Judy handed the leash to Doña Nereida. She had never been invited inside where Princess lived. Whenever she came back from her walks she waited around, hoping they would ask her in as well, but they never did. No one was invited into the back rooms where Don Osvaldo, Doña Nereida and Princess lived.

"Before you leave—Judy, here, have a piece of candy." Doña Nereida opened the cover of a glass display case and removed a small piece of coconut candy that sold for two cents apiece or three for a nickel. She handed it to Judy.

"Thank you," Judy said, taking the candy. She didn't much like it, but she ate it anyway.

"Osvaldo . . . Osvaldo," Doña Nereida called, "come

out here, I have to take Princess inside." Turning to Judy, she said, "Good-bye, Judy, see you later."

Judy smiled and left the store. She wished she could see where Princess lived. Shrugging her shoulders, she said to herself, Maybe tomorrow they'll ask me in.

"There's something wrong with these beans. Smell!" her mother said, handing the can of pork and beans to her children.

"Whew, yeah!" said Blanca. "They smell funny." She handed the can to William, who agreed, and then to Judy.

"They smell funny." Judy nodded.

"Can I smell too?" asked Angel. Judy handed him the can.

"Peeoowee . . ." he said, making a face. They all laughed.

"It's not funny," her mother said. "If these beans are rotten we could die." She held up the can. "Look—see that? The can is dented and swollen. Sure, he always gives us inferior merchandise. That no-good louse!" She shook her head. "We have to return them, that's all. You go, Judy, bring them back and tell him we want another can that's not spoiled."

"I have to walk Princess, Mami; send somebody else."

"You have to walk to the store and back here. Never mind Princess. Go on!"

"But I'll be too late then," Judy protested, thinking about her friends in the schoolyard.

"How would you like not to walk that mutt at all? What if I say that you cannot walk her any more," her mother said, looking severely at Judy.

Quietly, Judy got up and took the can of beans. "Mami,

they are already opened."

"Of course. How would I know otherwise if they are rotten? Here is the cover—just place it on top." She put the tin lid back on the opened can. "There . . . don't spill them and come right back here. I have to start supper."

"Can I walk Princess after I come back?"

"Yes," her mother said with exasperation. "Just come back with another can of beans!"

Judy rushed as quickly as she could, at the same time making sure that she did not spill the contents of the can.

"Here she is," said Doña Nereida when she saw Judy, "ready to take you out, Princess." As she fastened the leash, the dog barked and jumped, anxious to go out.

"Doña Nereida, I have to give you something first," Judy said.

"What?"

"Here is a can of beans that my brother William brought home before, and they are rotten." She put the can on the counter. "So my mother says could you please give us another can that is not spoiled."

Doña Nereida picked up the can and lifted the lid, sniffing the contents. "What's wrong with them?" she asked.

"They are rotten."

"Who says? They smell just fine to me. Wait a minute. Osvaldo! Osvaldo, come out here please!" Doña Nereida called loudly.

"What do you want? I'm busy." Don Osvaldo came out.

"Smell these beans. Go on." She handed her husband the opened can.

Don Osvaldo sniffed the contents and said, "They are fine. What's wrong?"

"Judy brought them—her mother wants another can. She says they are spoiled, that they are rotten."

"Tsk . . ." Don Osvaldo sighed and shook his head. "They are fine. They don't smell spoiled to me, or rotten. Besides, the can is opened. I can't exchange them if she opened the can already." He put the can back on the counter and covered it with the lid. "Here, take it back to your mother and tell her that there is nothing wrong with those beans. I can't change them."

Judy stood there and looked at the couple. She wanted to say that they smelled bad to her, too, but instead she said, "O.K., I'll tell her." She picked up the can of beans and returned home.

"What? Do you mean to tell me that he told you that there is nothing wrong with this can of beans?" Her mother's voice was loud and angry. "I don't believe it! Did he smell them?" she asked Judy.

"Yes," Judy said. "They both did."

Her mother shook her head. "I'm not putting up with this any more. This is the last time that thieving couple do this to me. Come on, Judy. You come with me. I'm taking back the beans myself. Let's see what he will tell me. You too, William; you come with us, since you were the one that bought the beans."

"Can I come too?" asked Angel.

"No," his mother answered, "stay with Blanca till I get back. I don't want you going up and down the stairs. And you, Blanca, start the rice. I'll be back in a little while."

Her mother walked in first, holding the can of beans. Judy and William followed.

"Don Osvaldo, I would like to return this can of beans," her mother said. Don Osvaldo was seated behind the counter, looking through his ledger. He put the book down.

"Mrs. Morales, there is nothing wrong with them beans," he said.

"Did you take a good smell? I sent Judy down before; and I cannot believe that after smelling them, you could refuse to exchange them for another can that is not spoiled!" She put the can on the counter.

Doña Nereida walked in, followed by Princess. When the dog saw Judy, she began to bark and jump up. "Shh . . ." said Doña Nereida. "Down! Get down, Princess, you are not going out right now. Maybe later. Down!" Princess sat down obediently, wagging her tail and looking at Judy. "What's happening here, Mrs. Morales?" she asked.

"It's about these beans. I refuse to accept them. That can is dented and swollen, that's how it got spoiled. Surely you don't expect me to feed this to my children."

"Why not?" said Doña Nereida. "They smell and look perfectly fine to me."

"Look, Mrs. Morales," said Don Osvaldo, "you probably opened the can and left it open a long time, and that's why they smell funny to you. But they are not spoiled, and I cannot give you another one or any credit for this."

"How could I know they are rotten unless I open up the can? Besides, I did not leave them open a long time. William just bought it here this afternoon," Mrs. Morales said and turned to her son. "Isn't that so, William?"

"Yes. I got them here and the can was already dented," said William.

"That doesn't mean anything," said Don Osvaldo. "You people opened them. There's nothing we can do."

Mrs. Morales looked at Don Osvaldo and Doña Nereida and smiled, remaining silent. After a moment, she asked, "You expect me to eat this and to feed this to my children?"

"You can do what you want with those beans," said Don Osvaldo. "It's not my affair."

"Will you at least give us some credit?" asked Mrs. Morales.

"We already told you, no!" said Doña Nereida. "Listen you are making a big thing over a can of beans when there is nothing wrong with them."

"Would you eat this, then?" asked Mrs. Morales.

"Of course," said Don Osvaldo.

"Certainly!" Doña Nereida nodded in agreement.

"O.K.," said Mrs. Morales, smiling, "I'll tell you what: You take them. A present from me to you. Eat them and enjoy them."

"All right." Don Osvaldo shrugged his shoulders. "If that's how you feel. It will be your loss. This can is not spoiled."

"Well then, I'll tell you what," said Mrs. Morales. "Why don't you feed it to Princess? Let Judy give it to her—a little present from us."

Don Osvaldo looked at his wife and she returned his glance, shrugging her shoulders.

"We are not going to eat them anyway, so why should they go to waste?" said Mrs. Morales. "Go on, Judy, take the beans and feed them to Princess." Turning toward

Doña Nereida, she asked, "Perhaps you could give Judy a little dish?" Doña Nereida did not answer, and looked with uncertainty at her husband. Mrs. Morales continued; this time she spoke to Don Osvaldo. "Why not? Don Osvaldo, if there is nothing wrong with the beans, then let's give them to Princess. She would probably enjoy them. It would be a treat."

"O.K.," he nodded, "sure. Nereida, get her blue dish from inside. If there is something wrong with the beans, Princess will not eat them."

His wife went into the back and returned, holding a bright-blue bowl with a happy white poodle on it.

"Here, Judy, you do it," said Mrs. Morales, looking at her daughter. "You give it to the dog. She'll take it from you."

Doña Nereida emptied the contents of the can into the bowl and gave it to Judy. Judy set it down on the floor near Princess.

"Here, girl, here's some beans for you," she said. Quickly, the little dog went over to the bowl and began to eat the beans, wagging her tail.

"See? Mrs. Morales, Princess is eating them beans. . . . There! Nothing was wrong with them. So you gave them away for nothing."

"That's all right, Don Osvaldo," Mrs. Morales responded. "It's not for nothing. Princess is enjoying the beans."

"Do you want another can of pork and beans?" asked Don Osvaldo, laughing. "I'm afraid I'll have to charge you, though!" His wife joined him in laughter as they both watched Princess finish the beans.

"No, thanks. I'll make do with what I have at home." Mrs. Morales turned to leave the store.

"Mami," said Judy, "can I walk Princess now?"

"No," her mother said, "you may not walk her now or later." As Judy followed her mother and brother out of the store, Don Osvaldo and Doña Nereida could still be heard laughing and commenting.

"How about tomorrow, Mami? Can I walk Princess tomorrow?" Judy persisted.

"We'll see . . . tomorrow," her mother answered.

At two the next morning, Osvaldo and Nereida Negrón were awakened by low whining sounds and grunts. When they got up to investigate, they found that Princess was having convulsions. Frightened, they tried to comfort the little dog by giving her water and then warm milk to drink. They even placed a hot-water bottle in her bed, but nothing seemed to help. The whining became softer and lower, until there was no sound at all. Princess lay in her small bed quietly, her eyes wide open, staring. The only visible sign of life was when her body jumped involuntarily, as if she had hiccups.

Don Osvaldo tried to calm his wife; she cried and wrung her hands, on the verge of hysteria. After a while, they decided the best thing to do was to take Princess to a veterinarian. Don Osvaldo found the names of several animal hospitals in the Yellow Pages, and after some telephone calls found one that would take Princess at this time of the morning. They wrapped the dog in a blanket and took a cab to the animal hospital. The doctor examined Princess and told them that her chances of surviving were slim. Whatever she had eaten was already digested and in her bloodstream. However, he promised to do his best and call them no matter what happened.

The Negróns returned to their store at six A.M., and at six thirty A.M. they received a phone call from the hospital informing them that Princess was dead. For a small fee they offered to dispose of the remains, and Don Osvaldo agreed.

Doña Nereida took to her bed, refusing to get up. Don Osvaldo opened his store a little late that day. Many of his credit customers had been patiently waiting outside; they had no place else to shop.

No one seemed to notice that Princess was not in the store. Don Osvaldo waited on his customers in silence, checking the back rooms every once in a while to see how his wife was. She remained in her bed, moaning softly and crying quietly.

As usual, that afternoon Judy went to the store to see Princess before going home. She entered and looked around for the little dog. Don Osvaldo was working behind the meat counter.

"Hi, Don Osvaldo," she said. "Where's Princess?"

"She's not here."

"Is she inside with Doña Nereida?" Judy asked and waited for a response. Don Osvaldo continued his work behind the meat counter, not speaking. Judy felt awkward and stepped up a little closer to the counter so that she could see Don Osvaldo. He was carefully cutting small, neat slices from a large side of beef and stacking them evenly on the other side of the chopping block.

After a short while, she said, "I'll be back, then, to walk her later. Good-bye, see you later," and turned to leave.

"Judy," Don Osvaldo said, "please tell your mother that when she sends for her groceries today, she should come herself." He paused. "Did you hear? Tell your mother to come for her groceries herself!"

"Yes," Judy replied, and went home.

Mrs. Morales entered Don Osvaldo's store accompanied by William and Judy.

"Be right with you, Mrs. Morales," Don Osvaldo said, and continued his work on the ledger.

The store was empty, and Judy looked around for Princess. In spite of her concern, she dared not ask Don Osvaldo about the little dog. Her mother's solemn attitude and Don Osvaldo's request this afternoon frightened her. For once, she wished her mother had not asked her to come along.

Don Osvaldo closed the ledger and looked at Mrs. Morales, staring at her without speaking. Finally, he asked, "Do you want anything? Can I get you something?"

"No, thank you," Mrs. Morales answered.

"Nothing?" he asked. "How about you, Judy? Do you want to take Princess for a walk?"

Judy looked at her mother, who reached out and pulled her daughter close to her.

"Do you want me to get her for you, Judy?" Don Osvaldo continued raising his voice loudly. "Do you want to take Princess for a little stroll? Well, answer! Answer!" he yelled.

Judy could feel her mother's body tensing up and trembling slightly.

111

"What do you want? You sent for me—what is it?" her mother asked.

"Do you know where she is? Where Princess is? She's dead. Dead. You killed her, that's what you did. You, too, Judy, both of you . . . all of you." Don Osvaldo's voice was angry. "She never did anything to you, to any of you. But you!" He pointed at Mrs. Morales. "You had to give that innocent animal, who never harmed you, something that would kill her, on spite! And you knew it—you knew it!"

"What do you want?" Mrs. Morales asked in a loud voice. "You have business with me? Tell me, or I'll leave!"

"Here . . ." Don Osvaldo said and pushed a white sheet of paper across the counter. "I don't want to touch you. Here is your bill. Pay up by the end of the week, or I'll take you to court. You get no more credit here!"

Mrs. Morales picked up the bill and examined it carefully. "I see, Don Osvaldo, that you have charged me for the beans." Her voice was shaking and she paused, clearing her throat. "I'm glad, real glad you did. It's a small price to pay for the life of my children. As God will judge!" Mrs. Morales made the sign of the cross. "You will get your money, don't worry, Don Osvaldo. It will be my pleasure."

In a moment, Mrs. Morales and her two children left the store.

Judy cried that night and on many other nights whenever she remembered Princess. She wished she had never given the beans to Princess. She stopped going to the schoolyard; she didn't know what to tell the kids there.

Her mother found a grocery store that sold to credit

customers. It was farther away—an extra fifteen-minute walk. They had two cats that Judy enjoyed playing with, but it was not the same.

Very often, she would pass by Don Osvaldo's grocery and glance inside, wondering if it had all been a dream and Princess were really in there waiting for her to come and play. She had spoken to several of the kids that shopped there, and all of them told her that the little dog was definitely not in the store. Still, there were times she would walk by and imagine Princess barking and wagging her tail, asking to be taken out to the schoolyard.

Two months went by, and one day, as Judy walked by Don Osvaldo's store on the way home, she heard someone call her name.

"Judy . . . psst, Judy . . . come over here."

She saw Doña Nereida calling her. "Come over here, Judy. . . . I want to talk to you." Judy moved slowly, with some trepidation. "Come on," Doña Nereida insisted. "I just want to see you a minute."

She followed the woman into the store. It was the first time she had set foot inside since the day that Don Osvaldo had spoken to her mother. She could hear her heart pounding, and she wondered what they wanted.

Don Osvaldo was busy waiting on a customer, and did not look in her direction.

"Come on with me," Doña Nereida whispered. "Come on!" Judy followed as she led her behind the counter and over to the back of the store.

They entered a medium-sized room with an old gas stove, a sink, a small refrigerator, and several kitchen cabinets.

The room was furnished with an old armchair in need of upholstering and a kitchen table with four chairs.

"Sit . . . sit down, Judy." They both sat down.

"I suppose you are wondering why I asked you in," she said. Judy nodded. "It's that . . . I just want to talk to you. About . . . Princess." Doña Nereida lowered her eyes and sighed. "You miss her too, I'll bet." Judy blushed. Being here with Doña Nereida embarrassed her. "Don't you?"

"Yes . . ." Judy said.

"She was so good; such a fine little dog. Almost like a person. We had her five years. She was so obedient." Doña Nereida paused and, choking back the tears, wiped her eyes. "It's not the same any more, you know. And he . . ." She gestured into the store. "He doesn't understand and expects me to forget! I can't. You understand, don't you?"

Judy nodded.

"See—I knew it. I told him. Judy—Judy knows. She loved Princess. She'll understand. I don't want another dog. You see, it wouldn't be fair to Princess. I have all her things, and he wants me to give them away!" She paused. "Would you like to see them? Would you?"

Judy shrugged her shoulders, feeling uncomfortable.

"Don't be shy. I know you want to see where Princess slept. Come on now." Doña Nereida stood up and took Judy into a small adjoining room. It had a large double bed and a dresser. Over in a corner was a child's colorful yellow-and-blue wardrobe unit. Next to it, on the floor, was what appeared to Judy to be a flat kind of wicker basket with a pillow. Inside was a rubber ball, a teething ring, and a toy telephone. "That's her little bed. We bought it at the pet shop on Third Avenue."

114

The room was stuffy and unkempt. Judy tried not to show her displeasure at the way the room smelled.

"It's been very hard on me." Judy wished that Doña Nereida would stop talking.

"Doña Nereida," Judy said, "I have to go home now. My mother is waiting."

"Of course. What will you think of me?" She led Judy back out through the front. Don Osvaldo was busy looking at his ledger. "Here, Judy. . . ." Doña Nereida reached into the glass display case and took a piece of white coconut candy. "Here."

"Thank you," said Judy.

"I know how you used to like this candy." She smiled.

"Good-bye," said Judy.

"Tomorrow. Come back tomorrow, Judy, and we'll talk some more!" She smiled.

"O.K.," Judy said, leaving the store. She put the candy in her mouth and decided that she definitely did not like it.

As she walked home, she felt strange about what had just happened. The back of the store didn't seem to have anything to do with the Princess she remembered—barking wildly, jumping, running, playing in the schoolyard, and chasing all the kids.

Judy made sure that on her way home from school, she did not pass by Don Osvaldo's store the next day, or any other day.

HERMAN AND ALICE

Part I

Alice turned over in bed, pulled the covers up over her head, and gently stroked her right shoulder where her mother had just poked her. Damn! she thought as she heard her mother's voice. Always nagging at me, do this and that —get up. . . . She heard her younger brother and sister getting ready for school. Wrapping her blanket even tighter around herself she could feel her belly press against her thighs as she curled up. It was hard to get used to this new feeling, a part of her body swelling up like a balloon. How nice, she said to herself, if I could let the air out and pop right back into being me again. At first she kept hoping it was some awful dream, and that in the morning she would awaken and get ready for school. She had given that up. No dream. She knew that now, but it was hard getting used to.

"Alice, get up, will you? Muchacha, how many times I gotta call you, eh?" Her mother's voice was right over her. She lowered the covers and looked up at her mother.

"Ma, I don't feel good again. Mami, please let me stay in bed for a while."

"Oh . . . no. . . . No, chica, not again! You don't feel well; sleep all day and then you wanna stay up late? Too bad! Come on, get up. You feel better when you get up. It will pass; come on."

"That's what you said two months ago."

"Well, it will pass sooner or later. I oughta know, I been pregnant enough times. Come on, you are not the only one going to have a child. Even la Virgen María suffered, so get up and help! This is no hotel."

Closing her eyes, Alice could smell the boiled milk and coffee her mother was making for breakfast. A wave of nausea hit her, and she sat up. Any strong cooking odor seemed to make her ill, especially early in the morning. No use arguing, she thought, and decided to get up.

In the kitchen, the children were just finishing breakfast. Alice's mother was preparing her stepfather's lunch.

"Please go down to the store, Alice, and get me some mayonnaise for Luis's lunch."

"In a minute, Ma," Alice said.

"No, not in a minute. Now! I gotta leave for work soon."

"Why can't one of them go?" Alice asked, looking at her brother and sister.

"They gotta go to school. They cannot be late. What are you doing that's so great? Eh . . . Miss? You gonna lay around all day, reading magazines, then eat, then sleep? You not doing nothing; you go!" Her mother's voice was loud and angry.

"Ma, it's still early. All the kids are on the way to school. I don't wanna go out! Please, Ma, let Tony or Fela go. I am not—"

117

"Stop!" her mother interrupted. "Stop that nonsense. What is the secret? Everybody knows already. What are you hiding? You pregnant, that's all! You not the first and you not gonna be the last."

"I haven't any clothes. I look ridiculous, Ma. Nothing fits." Tony and Fela began to laugh. "Shut up!" Alice smacked Tony on the back of the head.

"Ouch! Ma . . . Mami," he screamed.

"Basta! Alice, leave him alone. Yes, you are ridiculous. Don't take it out on him. Go find the Prince Charming responsible for your looks. What are we supposed to do? Pay for your good time? You don't work; you don't do nothing but complain. Now you wanna stay here? Caramba, you work like everybody else!" Her mother was screaming, and Tony continued to whine. "Shut up, Tony!"

"Quiet." A man's voice was heard from one of the bedrooms in the apartment. "Every day the same basura. Let me get some sleep! How am I gonna get up for work? God damn it!"

"You see?" whispered her mother. "Luis woke up. It's your fault again. Now get your coat on and get going."

Alice left the kitchen. She could feel the anger surging in her and the tears filling her eyes.

"A medium-size jar of mayonnaise . . . and charge it," she heard her mother's voice.

She opened her bedroom closet, pushing Fela's clothes aside. Maybe if I put on a sweater under my raincoat, she thought, it'll look better. It was a warm Indian summer day, and she felt foolish putting on a heavy pullover, but without hesitating she put it on. She draped the raincoat over

118

her shoulders and stood before the mirror. Alice looked at herself for a moment, and then decided it was better to put on the coat. She wished she had sunglasses. Fela had broken the last pair she had. What a pest, she thought, always taking my things. Looking around at the small room she shared with her little sister, she felt guilty. Her mother had said she could have this room for herself when the baby was born. Fela would have to go into Tony's room.

"Look at the trouble you cause, Alice. Your sister will soon get her period, and now she has to sleep in the same room with Tony."

Alice heard the front door slam. They've left for school, she thought jealously. She remembered when she was Fela's age. What fun, she thought, playing games after school— jump rope, hide-and-go-seek—and no worries. Meeting my friends . . .

"You finally going to the store?" her mother called out. "Get also a quarter pound of American cheese. You hear? Alice . . . Alice? Answer!"

"Yessss!" Alice screamed. Her mother came out of the kitchen.

"You . . . making trouble, that's all you know. Shut up before you wake up Luis again. You're always making it worse for me with Luis. Maybe you can't get a husband but I intend to keep mine. . . . I'm sick of your . . ."

Her mother's voice faded as Alice slammed the front door and headed down the stairs. "I hate her, I hate her," Alice whispered to herself, quickly running down the stairs. She hesitated by the stoop steps for a moment. The street was empty. Pulling the raincoat snugly around her and putting both hands in her pockets, she looked straight ahead and walked at a fast pace to the corner grocery.

Herman folded his copy of the *Daily News* and dumped the dirty breakfast dishes into a pan of warm soapy water in the kitchen sink. He checked his watch, making sure he was on schedule. Raining again, he thought, looking out of the kitchen window. He put on his raincoat and brown fedora; for a moment he was unsure as to whether or not he should take his umbrella, then decided against it.

"It's not raining that hard," he said out loud, breaking the silence in the apartment. Herman made sure all the lights were out, except for the small lamp in the foyer. He checked his wallet, his keys, change for the subway. Satisfied, he opened his front door, stepped outside, and began carefully locking his apartment. All those robberies and muggings— just awful, he thought, and now the neighborhood is worse than ever with all those dope users. He felt more secure since he had installed a new safety lock. At one time he had even considered keeping a dog, but there would be no one to look after it during the day, and he had abandoned the idea.

After they had robbed the old woman, Doña Rosa, and her niece, Herman had been determined to move. But where to? Rents were too high in good neighborhoods; and besides, Herman reasoned, what about his being Puerto Rican? That was another problem. When they find out you're Puerto Rican they won't rent to you. Right now, it was best to stay here and be very careful and alert, he thought, what with such a change in the neighborhood—

120

good people moving out. Shaking his head, he realized he was mumbling out loud again.

When he reached the ground floor, he noticed someone standing by the wall near the mail boxes. It was that girl— her name was Alice—and he remembered the screaming he had heard this morning. That family was always fighting. Poor kid, she's pregnant. Another mess, he thought. As he walked by her, he turned and smiled.

"How are you? Another rainy day again. Well, thank heaven it's still warm. Better than snow . . ." Herman hesitated, waiting for a response.

Alice looked at him, her eyes red from crying, and she nodded.

"Don't you hate the snow? Terrible. So cold, and the landlord gives us less heat each winter. . . . At least it seems that way."

Alice nodded again and said nothing.

"Well, I must be off; have to catch the train—miserable subways," he said.

Alice closed her eyes. Her face began to twitch and she started to sob. At first the sobs were barely audible and her body shook. Herman was startled and impulsively stepped back, a little frightened. Alice continued to cry with her eyes shut. The sobs became louder, tears ran down her cheeks, and she opened her mouth slightly, letting forth a low, painful whine. Herman stared at her, not moving.

"Are you all right?" he asked. She did not answer, and for a moment he felt foolish. Her eyes were wide open; they were dark brown, almost like black liquid, spilling clear, transparent tears.

121

As Herman looked at Alice, he remembered a young boy in Puerto Rico. He had come one day to Herman's house to beg for food. He lived with his family in a leper colony, but he looked normal. Everyone was frightened of the lepers; they were wretched, miserable, and poor; some hideously deformed. People would throw money and food at them, making sure they stayed at a distance. They would lock up their doors and windows, afraid of the dreaded disease. The boy had come alone, and at first Herman's family had fed the boy. When they saw the rest of his family, they screamed, forcing him to leave. They picked up stones and sticks, striking him. He cried, asking for pity as they abused him. Herman remembered the boy as he had stared at his tormentors. His eyes were dark like two whirlpools—as if no one could see where the sadness ended. Herman felt a shortness of breath: the same eyes! She has the same eyes, just like that boy, he thought. Herman stepped up to Alice and gently touched her shoulder.

"It's too much . . . isn't it?" he asked very softly. She put her head on his chest and quietly cried some more. After a while, Herman gave her his white handkerchief.

"Sorry, Mr. Aviles. I'm sorry," she said.

"There is nothing to be sorry about." They were quiet for a moment.

"I have to bring up this for my mother," Alice said, holding out the brown paper bag she carried.

"I have to catch my train." Herman smiled. Alice nodded, trying to smile.

"O.K.," she said.

"Well," Herman hesitated, then quickly said, "come to

see me if you like. I'm not doing anything tonight. You can have a drink—or, well . . . I mean something. A glass of milk or tea or coffee."

"If you want me to." Alice looked at him with surprise and shrugged her shoulders. "O.K."

"Ooops, look at the time," Herman said, looking at his watch. "Bendito, I better get going. I'm late."

"Hey—what time?" Alice called after him.

"In the evening, any time. No fuss, just any time," Herman answered and walked swiftly to the subway. He felt somewhat ridiculous inviting the child to his apartment. What can we talk about? he asked himself. But somehow a feeling of excitement was beginning to take over and he felt slightly elated and giddy.

Alice held Herman's handkerchief as she went up the stairs. Mr. Aviles, she said to herself, repeating his name several times. She realized that she had never really thought about him in any way except as a person who lived in the building. Everyone likes him, she thought. He was polite and quiet, and he lived alone. She remembered her mother saying that he was the kind of person who gave the building a good name. "He is a better quality person and has wonderful manners. He's educated, not one of those ordinarios, those loudmouths that are coming here from Puerto Rico to El Bronx."

Before opening the door to her apartment, Alice tucked the handkerchief into one of her coat pockets.

"Alice? Is that you? I'm waiting to leave. I don't wanna be late." Alice walked into the kitchen.

"Fix yourself something."

123

"I'm not hungry," Alice said, sulking.

"I have to go to work, Alice. I can't stop to make your breakfast—I'm late." Her mother worked swiftly as she packed sandwiches into a black metal lunch box.

"I'm not asking you to make me nothing."

"Mira," her mother said, "I'm sorry I hollered at you before, but . . . things are hard enough for me without—without my having to be after you to do things all the time."

Alice walked out of the kitchen.

"We'll talk about it when I get home from work. Later."

Alice felt very tired; she was always tired. It seems I got no energy, she thought. The front door slammed, and she knew her mother had gone to work. She searched in her coat pocket for the handkerchief. She lay down and put the white handkerchief up to her nose, inhaling deeply. It smells clean, so clean, she thought, just like him, nice. Like Mr. Aviles.

Standing before the closed door, Alice looked at the nameplate above the bell. It read HERMAN E. AVILES. She felt the nervousness in the pit of her stomach. At first she was afraid of meeting someone in the hall or on the stairway. So far so good, she had thought with a sense of relief, but now as she stood there she was scared all over again. If she went back upstairs, Alice knew she would spend another evening with Tony and Fela. Another night of arguments and boredom, no thanks, she said to herself, pressing the bell for a good long moment. She heard footsteps on the other side. The door opened partially and she saw Mr. Aviles.

"Buenas—" she heard him say as he released the chain and opened the door wide. Standing before her, he smiled. "Come on in, Alice." She followed him down the narrow foyer and into the living room.

"Well," he said, "here we are."

"This is nice. You got a real nice place," said Alice.

"It's small, but then it's only for me." They both remained silent, and the faint sounds of the traffic in the streets seemed to become clear and louder. After a while, Herman said, "For heaven's sake, forgive me for being a bad host. Let me have your coat."

"Thank you, Mr. Aviles."

"How about something to drink?" he asked. "And please, Alice, call me Herman. Otherwise I'll feel like your grandfather. Now, do you want a Coke, or ginger ale, or I also have milk."

"Coke is good, Mr. Aviles . . . Herman." Alice smiled.

"That's better. Just sit down on the couch and make yourself at home. I'll be right back. You want a little ice in your glass?"

"Yes . . . good," Alice said.

The room was different from most places she had ever been in. The couch was a grey tweed. There were two matching armchairs with some dark green-and-black throw pillows. The floor was covered by a large grey cotton shag rug. A bookcase contained some books, vases with dried flowers, a plaster figure of a nude male torso, and a painted wooden carving of a matador flinging his red cape at a charging bull. Before her was a low wood-and-glass coffee table. Alice thought of her apartment. What a difference.

125

Everything is so nice and new and clean here. Closing her eyes for a moment, she opened them quickly, satisfied that this was really happening. Herman walked in with a small tray in his hand and Alice started to rise.

"No . . . sit, sit down," Herman said, and placed the tray with two glasses of Coke on the table. "Here," he said, handing her a glass. "Take a napkin."

"Thank you," Alice said.

"Well." Herman picked up his glass. "Here's to you."

"Here's to you, too," Alice responded. They both drank some soda. "You got a real beautiful place, Mr. Aviles—I mean Herman. It's real sharp."

"Thank you, Alice." He sat down in one of the armchairs. "I'm glad you like it. Have some cheese and crackers," he said, holding the dish toward her. Alice took a couple of crackers and some olives.

"Do you got a television?" she asked. "I don't see none."

"Yes, I do, but it's in the bedroom. I put it on at night and I can relax in bed and enjoy it."

"Oh." Alice smiled. After a short while she asked, "Do you work very far from here?"

"It's far, but not bad. It's a straight ride downtown on one train to Bowling Green station. I work for a steamship company."

"Oh," Alice said, impressed.

"I have been with them ever since I came to El Bronx from Puerto Rico. Seven years. Dios mío! Time goes by so fast. So . . ." Herman hesitated. "I'm boring you."

"No, you're not," Alice said. "I like to hear about it. Honest!"

126

"Well," Herman continued, "when I got out of the Army I came here, and I took a course in business under the G.I. Bill, at the Latin American Clerical Institute, and got this job. At first I was just a typist, but then I was able to advance and . . ." Alice vaguely listened as Herman spoke; she couldn't believe that Mr. Aviles was talking to her and telling her all about his life. No one really knew anything about him. She thought about her mother. I'll bet she wouldn't believe me. She was glad she had not told anyone about her visit. ". . . I haven't found another job that I would care to take. So as long as there is some room for advancement, I might as well stay where I am." Herman stopped speaking and looked at Alice, expecting a reply.

"Do you have a mother and father?" she asked.

"Yes, as a matter of fact I do. In Arecibo, Puerto Rico. You probably never heard of it. It's a small town. Anyway, it has been seven years since I have seen them. That is a long time—too long."

"You got any brothers and sisters?" Alice asked, and then blushed. "Look, you don't have to answer my questions. I am probably getting too nosy anyway. I'm sorry."

"No," Herman laughed. "No, that's O.K. I don't mind. I have two married brothers and one married sister and they all have children. In fact, one of my nieces just had a baby herself. You probably think I'm an old man. Well, you are right, but I won't tell you my age. So don't ask me!"

"I don't—I don't think you're old. I really don't. Please . . . I think you're nice." Alice felt herself blushing and looked away, wishing she hadn't said that.

"You are a very nice person yourself, Alice," Herman

127

said. After a brief silence, he asked, "How about some more cheese and crackers, or more soda?"

"O.K., I'll take more Coke." Herman took her glass and went back into the kitchen.

Alice remembered what he had said, and her heart jumped. He said I was very nice, she thought, and hoped he really meant it. Maybe he just feels sorry for me, that's why he said it. She became aware of her clothes. Her blouse was very tight and her checkered skirt was stained and too short. A piece of the hem was coming apart and a loose thread hung down her leg, almost touching her old brown moccasins. She looked at her stomach; it seemed at that moment to protrude further and further. I should leave—I look ridiculous, she said to herself. I wonder if he is laughing at me? Just like all of them, laughing behind my back. I gotta get out of here! She was about to stand when Herman walked in. He smiled and handed her a glass. She put the cold drink to her lips, closed her eyes, and sipped some of the sweet liquid. With her eyes shut, she spoke softly but clearly.

"I'm gonna have a baby, you know. . . . I'm pregnant—everybody knows it. I am not married and I'm not gonna get married. I don't even go to school no more. I got kicked out." Alice opened her eyes and looked at Herman. "That's who I am, you know. You should know who I am."

They looked at each other and Herman said, "It doesn't matter to me. It's none of my business."

"I just want you to know." Alice's voice was almost inaudible. "I just want . . . you to know that I am . . . this way and the whole neighborhood knows about it. They talk about me, and maybe I should go."

"Alice, it does not mean anything to me what the people say. You don't have to leave. De veras, honest, I like you."

"Don't feel sorry for me. I can take care of myself, you know. I don't need nobody feeling sorry."

"I don't feel sorry," Herman said. "Don't go—unless you want to. First, finish your drink."

"I think I better go," Alice said, not moving.

"Why don't you finish your drink, then, before you go?"

Alice quickly swallowed the rest of the soda. He must think I am really ridiculous, she thought, and put the glass down.

"Would you like to see the rest of the apartment?" he asked.

Nodding, Alice followed Herman out of the living room.

"This is the kitchen. It's not very large but I can eat in here."

"It's nice."

"Here," Herman said, "is the bedroom." Alice saw a blond-wood bedroom set, complete with headboard. The windows had green satin drapes from ceiling to floor. A matching green satin bedspread covered the large double bed. On the wall, over the bed, hung a white crucifix with white rosary beads wrapped around it. A portable television was at the foot of the bed.

"That's really beautiful," Alice said. "I seen that same bedroom set down on Third Avenue in the window of Hearn's Department Store. Exactly the same thing, man—I swear!"

Alice followed Herman back toward the front door.

"Let me get your coat, Alice." Herman held it for her.

129

"Listen, Mr. Avil—Herman, I got your handkerchief and I'll wash it and bring it to you, O.K.?"

"That's all right, Alice, I can take care of it."

"No, I want to. I'll wash it. Thanks . . . listen, thanks a lot for everything. I had a good time. I really did."

"I had a good time too. Come again, O.K.?"

"O.K. When?"

"Any time you want to, Alice." Herman smiled. "To-morrow?"

"Good. That way I can bring you your handkerchief."

Herman opened the front door and Alice hesitated, afraid that someone might be in the hallway. It was quiet, and she darted up the stairs. I just hope I didn't make an idiot fool of myself with Mr. Aviles, she thought. Well, now he knows, anyway.

"You back?" She heard her mother. "Why didn't you tell me you was going out? I needed some things from the candy store. I had to go myself, because Tony went to a friend's house and I don't want Fela going out late by herself. You could have told me."

"Crap again!" Alice whispered. She walked into her bedroom and sat on her bed. Her mother followed and stood in the doorway.

"Where were you, eh? Alice?"

"No place."

"Mira, Alice, we gotta make some plans, you know." Her mother sat next to Alice. "It's gonna be time before you know it. You are almost six months."

"Ma, I'm tired."

"Look, you are gonna have to make plans. What do you think a baby is? Now we are due to go to the welfare agency

130

next Tuesday. We gotta see what they can give us and what you gonna need. I have to take time out from work; that is costing money. You know that?"

"I'll get a job, Mama."

"Ha! Qué linda. Bendito, you gonna get a job! With a baby? Maybe later, when you can leave it with a woman. But I gotta work and Luis has to have his rest. You know he will be on the night shift most of the time, like always. You better start to think, you hear?"

"All right, Mama," Alice said.

"O.K.," her mother said, "good. You got your clinic card. . . . And we cannot tell them that I am working now, because they won't give us much and God knows you need everything. When we get there, I want you to know what to tell them. So that means that we are five in the family, but you are not Luis's child and any help from the baby's father is out of the question. We can give you the room, but everything else . . . maybe they will give assistance. After you have the baby, you go to work with me at la factoría, but we cannot say that. . . ." Alice listened and nodded in agreement with everything she said. Who cares? I don't give a damn. I wish she would hurry up and finish and shut up, she thought.

Alice felt a slight movement in her and was startled. This was the third time it had happened in two days. Until very recently, she could not believe that something real and alive was inside her. Now she realized it was true.

"Mami . . . it moved. . . . I felt it, the baby inside, Ma." Alice put her hands on her belly. "Look, right here."

"Really?" Her mother smiled. "Well, Alice, now you know. You have felt life inside you—you are no longer a

131

child. I had to start my life as a woman the same way, Alice —with you." Her mother stopped speaking and gently put her arms around Alice. It was the first time in years that she remembered her mother holding her. "I had hoped for you it might have been different," her mother whispered. Alice did not answer; the feeling of shame choked her, and she began to cry.

"Ma . . . I'm sorry, Mami, I really am sorry. Really, Mami." Her mother held her quietly and listened as Alice tried to speak. After a while, her mother released her.

"I know, mi hijita," she said. "I know you are sorry. I am too, Alice, but it's too late now. Because now, you see, you can be sorry for the rest of your life." Her mother stood up and walked out of the room. Alice lay down and tried to control the sobbing. She reached under her pillow and pressed the white handkerchief against her mouth. She closed her eyes and made believe she was in Mr. Aviles's bedroom, sleeping on the beautiful bed surrounded by the pretty things in that beautiful room.

Herman put the box of crackers away and cleared the dishes. What a mess, poor little thing, all alone. I'll bet that family is no help at all. I wonder if she is receiving medical help. Honestly, these people, a bunch of ignorantes, and they just keep making babies and more babies and being more miserable. She is so proud, too. Herman continued to talk to himself and then stopped abruptly, realizing that this was the first time in a very long while that he was involved with another person.

He thought about Daniel; not since Daniel. What was it? he wondered, six months? . . . Dios mío, more; almost a year since he had last seen him. During those first weeks it had been awful, but now he seldom thought about him. He had been glad when Daniel quit the company and went to work elsewhere. It would have been unbearable if he had to see him every day, knowing it was all over, finished. Beautiful Daniel, so sweet, so loving. Oh well, Herman remembered, he had never promised anything.

At first it was just lunch. Herman had taken him home and the relationship began.

"I'm not getting tied to anybody, Herman," Daniel had warned him at the very beginning. "I don't know what I wanna do . . . and I wanna be free to split, if that's what suits me. . . ."

"No demands," Herman had said. "I promise—you can go when you want. But for now let's just be together."

They had seen each other exactly sixteen months. That had been a happy time for Herman. He thought about the seven years he had spent here. Three relationships that had any meaning; the rest were nothing. He had bought the bedroom set for Daniel, with the green drapes and bedspread; green was his favorite color, and Herman wanted him to have it. Well, it didn't matter anyway. After Daniel, he had given up looking for that someone. Lately, he had been thinking of going back to Arecibo, if only for a visit, to see his parents. Perhaps he could get a job in San Juan and settle down there. He could never live in Arecibo. In that town, Herman thought, with all its petty gossip, life had become a nightmare. Even the Army was a blessing; anything to get away from that stifling environment. Everyone trying to get him married.

He got ready for bed, lit a cigarette, and lay down.

Maybe, he thought, I'll get something sweet for her. Cake. On Nassau Street, near work, they have that wonderful bakery—yes, she would like that. She looks so raggedy. Herman shook his head. She probably doesn't have any clothes. He inhaled deeply and blew out the smoke. She is so young, he thought, just a baby.

Herman got out of bed and stood before the mirror. He looked carefully at himself. I'm getting greyer, he thought. It's thinning; every week I lose more hair, he said to himself, depressed. I hate bald men. I hate being old. In a couple of more years I'll be forty. Forty! Well . . . Herman stood back a bit from the mirror. He was proud of his figure, nice and slim; still the same size that he had been at nineteen. He had not done his push-ups lately and had not renewed his membership at the YMCA.

I am gonna do that soon—I will renew my membership and start my exercises, he said to himself with conviction. I could pass for thirty if I dyed my hair. Perhaps I'll do that before it gets too grey.

Herman lay down again, feeling better than he had felt in months.

Part II

Alice had showered, shampooed, and doused herself generously with toilet water. In her room, she took out her new outfit. Her mother had bought her one dressy outfit and a casual skirt with two cotton tops.

"It won't do to have you going out with a man like Mr.

134

Aviles looking like that," her mother had said. "What would he think of us? After all, we are not a bunch of jíbaros!"

When she first planned to tell her mother about Herman and the visits, Alice was frightened, not knowing what her response would be. Her mother's reaction was, at first, disbelief.

"If you don't wanna believe me, Ma, then go ask him yourself. That's where I been going evenings. It's been already two weeks."

Impressed, her mother asked her many questions until she seemed satisfied that Alice was telling the truth. Then she had become excited.

"Well, Alice, you can consider yourself lucky to have such a fine person interested in you. He is so educated. I hope you act proper."

Alice put on her new outfit. It felt good wearing something new and something that fit. Today, Herman was taking her to see the Empire State Building and then out to eat in a restaurant. She had never been inside the Empire State Building, but she had heard about it from the kids in school. Man, I can't wait! she said to herself.

Tony and Fela were still at Sunday Mass. Alice never went to Mass any more; she knew everyone would be there. I hope they don't get back early, she said to herself. They might embarrass me. When the children found out that she was seeing Herman, they had laughed and called him an old man. Alice had been furious and complained to her mother. "Mr. Aviles is a mature man of the world, not old," her mother had said. "Why, in Puerto Rico it is often the custom for a young girl to go out with a mature man." Alice

135

nonetheless felt self-conscious. Before the children had mentioned his age, she had not thought of Herman as being old.

She looked in the mirror, admiring herself. She liked the contrast of her dark hair against the lightness of her dress. Alice heard the bell and her mother open the front door.

She was surprised to see both her mother and stepfather in the living room with Herman. Luis never got up early, especially on Sunday. He was fully dressed and her mother had on her best Sunday clothes.

"Luis Antonio Quiñones . . . mucho gusto," her step-father said.

"Herman Edmundo Aviles," Herman replied with a polite nod.

"Alice," her mother said, "Mr. Aviles is already here waiting for you."

"Hello," Alice said.

"Alice," Herman said, smiling at her, "you look very, very nice."

"Mr. Aviles, would you like to sit and have something?" her mother asked.

"No . . . thank you very much, Mrs. Quiñones; I had a very late breakfast today."

"Well, you got no rain, anyway," her mother smiled. "So you got some luck today."

"Yes," Herman answered, "the sun is out. We better get going—we have a long day ahead. But Mrs. Quiñones, I promise I will not keep her out late. I'll bring her home at a decent hour."

"Oh, please don't worry. Really, Mr. Aviles, we got all

the confidence that you will take care of her. Isn't that so, Luis?"

"Yes," Luis responded, "we appreciate you taking an interest in Alice. You welcomed to take her out any time. Any time."

Two women were on the stoop steps as they walked by, and Alice felt her face flush. She knew they were whispering and staring. Let them look, she thought; I don't care who sees us. There was a feeling of freedom within her. There was no reason to feel ashamed, she thought, and tightened her grip on Herman's arm as they walked toward the subway. For the first time Alice felt like his equal. Yes, she thought, Ma's right; he is mature, not old.

Herman had enjoyed himself immensely with Alice, and that evening he thought about her. There is so much to see in New York and this kid has never been anywhere. She's never left El Bronx, he thought; just like so many of the kids back home who have never even been to San Juan. God! He wanted to take her out to show her things; teach her. He smiled and recalled her astonishment and pleasure at everything. Like a second chance at living, he said to himself. I feel alive again. Herman remembered the people who looked at them in the subway and in the restaurant. No one had said anything, and no one had stared at them; just another couple, a guy and his young pregnant wife. Wife . . . my wife? Herman chuckled out loud, shaking his head. He had never had a physical relationship with a woman. Even now, the very idea repelled him, and he shrugged his shoulders as if shaking off a chill.

But Alice. Alice was different, he thought. Just a kid, and pregnant as well. She is so fragile and sensitive, so easily hurt. He found himself angry at her parents. That man, so indifferent, and that mother ready to throw her out. They don't deserve a girl like Alice, he thought. Tomorrow he would pick up the book on prenatal care for her; she had promised to read it. He had to pick up a jar of multiple vitamins; he was sure she was not eating properly.

Because Alice spent most of her time in Herman's apartment, he had given her a set of keys. They had supper together just about every day; they went shopping and to the movies. Alice's family had stayed at a distance. He disliked them and was grateful that they did not interfere in his relationship with Alice.

Tonight, Alice was preparing supper; she hummed along with the music on the radio as she worked in the kitchen. Neighbors in the building had commented to her mother about her new relationship. Alice laughed at the idea that people might assume that she and Herman were going steady. She wondered if Herman knew about it and how he felt about her. I wonder if he'll like me once the baby is born. She felt better when she remembered what he had called her.

"Alice, you look beautiful. There is nothing more beautiful and sacred than motherhood." She smiled, moved, as she recalled his words. "Madonna de mis sueños . . . madonna of my dreams."

He was always gentle, always good; he really cares, she thought. Not like Stevie. Alice leaned against the sink. She tried not to remember, but in spite of herself she could not help thinking about Stevie and feeling confused and ashamed. He was engaged to Diana; everybody knew it. They were going to be married in June. It was so stupid! Alice thought. It happened only twice. The first time it was painful and she had cried; the second time it was almost as bad, except she had felt numb. Diana was popular. She had become friendly with Alice and some of the younger girls in the neighborhood. When Diana had invited her to the engagement party, Alice was impressed, feeling very grown up. All the other kids were at least sixteen or older. Everybody at the party drank too much, and there was a big fight. Diana and Stevie broke off their engagement. Alice was high when Stevie made a pass, and she responded, flattered that he noticed her. Later that night they met on the stairway leading to the roof. It happened so quickly. She felt nothing except fear and pain. Stevie was drunk and held her tightly. For a moment, she struggled to leave, but he covered her mouth with his hand, warning her not to cry or scream because someone might hear them. Alice now found herself crying as she remembered how Stevie forced his way into her. "How dumb!" she whispered out loud.

The second time she had cut school and agreed to meet him at his apartment, Diana and Stevie had made up. But she felt pleased and surprised that Stevie could want her. Once again she let him do what he wanted. . . . This time she didn't attempt to resist. The pain was not so bad the second time, but the numbness was awful. When Stevie finished, Alice did not want to look at him. She never wanted to see him again.

Nothing had changed. Not even herself. Alice had changed least of all.

She felt a sharp kick inside her belly and realized she still had to cook supper. Well, she said to herself, I'm glad he's married to Diana. I hate him. She told her mother it was a married man, and that the man had long since moved to another state.

Alice had never been a good student. She did not miss school and never even planned to finish. But she missed her friends, especially Olga. Olga Fuentes had been her best friend since second grade. After Alice left school, Olga's mother would not let them see each other. It had been very lonely until Herman. She stopped for a moment and rubbed her back. Lately, her back ached whenever she stood for a long time. She looked at the salad she was making; Herman had taught her just how to do it. She wondered how he felt about her. Does he like me that way? Alice asked herself. He has never even kissed me . . . or touched me. Alice felt both relieved and disappointed by this. Still, she wanted to know. I have to know how he feels, she said to herself. Maybe tonight I'll ask him. I'll just tell him what people are saying about us, that's all.

Everything was done, and by the time Herman got home, supper would be ready to serve. Herman had put the television into the living room so that Alice could watch it whenever she wanted. Christmas commercials were on. God, she thought, only a couple of weeks till Christmas! Man, am I broke. Welfare would not give her anything until after the baby was born. Awful people, she almost said out loud. All those questions, making you feel like two cents. She decided not to think about Welfare. She was just going to watch television and wait for Herman.

After supper, Alice and Herman sat in the living room as usual. He had bought her a new popular teen fashion magazine, and she thumbed through it looking at the clothes and fashion articles. Herman smoked his cigarette and listened to Alice.

"Herman, look," she said, pointing to an ad in the magazine. "See? That's some sharp outfit. I wish I could wear them clothes. I'll have to wait—right now I look like an elephant." She giggled. After a short while Alice looked at Herman.

"Herman? Would you like to feel the baby? It's moving again." Herman moved over and, sitting close to Alice, put his hands on her stomach.

"Ave María! You got an acrobat inside there, Alice, I swear," Herman said, laughing.

"It didn't even let me sleep last night, jumping around. I don't think it sleeps at night." She laughed. "I wonder if it'll be a boy or a girl. I still want a girl, Herman."

"Let it be healthy, Alice, that's what's important."

"Herman?" Alice asked, pausing. "Herman, do you know people in the building are talking about us? You and me, I mean. . . . My mother told me."

"I told you, Alice, I don't listen to gossip."

"I know that. But, well, they are saying that you and me, we . . ." Alice felt herself blush. "You know? Like there is something more."

"Alice, I don't . . ." Herman stood up, then decided to sit down again. "Alice, I don't feel that way about you."

141

"It's because I'm pregnant. Right? I look awful." She felt the tears coming to her eyes, and bit her lips, trying not to cry.

"No, Alice, honest. It's not that. You look just fine." Herman turned away and then asked, "How do you feel about me, Alice? Do you . . . feel that way?"

She could feel the color coming into her cheeks; her face seemed to be burning. Not looking at Herman, she answered very softly, "I don't know, Herman. I don't think so, only . . . I just don't know what to think sometimes."

"I'm going to tell you something, Alice. I cannot . . . feel that way about you. I just don't feel that way about—about women. It's not you."

Alice looked at Herman. "What?"

"I don't feel that way about women," he said, looking directly at her.

"You don't?" Alice asked, bewildered.

"Alice . . . I like you very much, and I even think— maybe it's crazy—but I think we could be happy together, as long as . . . well, as long as there is . . . nothing but friendship."

"Nothing but friendship?" Alice's voice was just under a whisper.

"No sex, Alice. I can't have sex with a woman." Herman's face was ashen. Alice remained quiet and looked away from him. "Alice?" Herman waited for a response. "Alice, did you hear what I said?"

She felt numb, a familiar sense of numbness once more. She nodded and, without looking at him, asked, "Do you like guys, Herman?"

142

"Alice, please, there's no use—"

"Please, Herman," she interrupted, speaking softly. "Just let me know if you like guys. That's all."

"Alice—look, it doesn't mean that much to me. In the past it was with . . . guys—but it . . . I don't really enjoy it. Sex is not important, and the past—well, the past is over. I really want to be with you. Just Alice. I can't . . . I . . . please—do you understand? We can be friends, we can try for something else." Herman stopped speaking and looked intently at Alice. He couldn't say any more, and he waited.

Alice turned and looked directly at him. She said, "I don't care about sex either, Herman. Honest," she said.

"O.K.," he said, smiling. They looked at each other for a while and then both of them laughed giddily.

That evening they went window-shopping. As they walked arm in arm, Herman felt at peace with himself. And now he was glad he had been honest. He looked at her, feeling closer. Alice looked at Herman. A let-down feeling kept annoying her, and she wondered if something wasn't her fault after all.

There was really nothing else to do; this was the only way as far as Herman was concerned. The idea of Alice living with the baby in that crowded apartment with those people was intolerable.

"What do you think, Alice?" Herman asked. "The sooner we get married, the easier it will be to arrange things for the baby. You are due next month."

"All right." Alice had nodded, pleased.

The apartment was now her home. My real home, she

thought. Herman had taught her how to care for things. He took her to the movies, shopping, and out to eat. Whenever she wanted something, Herman got it for her.

Herman told his co-workers. They all chipped in and bought an electric broiler. He told some of them that his bride-to-be was pregnant and that he would be a father in a month. They whispered in amazement; Herman was so quiet; who would have thought . . . ? Well, you see . . . one never can tell!

Alice was still fifteen, and therefore considered a minor by law. Her mother readily gave her consent. Herman gave his age as thirty. Father García performed a quick religious ceremony in the rectory of St. Anselm's Catholic Church, not far from where they lived. Herman insisted on taking everyone out for a large Chinese dinner. Patricia Quiñones and her husband, Luis, with their two children, Tony and Fela, were the only ones joining the couple in celebration. After dinner they headed home, and each family went to its own apartment.

That night, Alice had her wish—one that she had been nurturing since her first visit to the apartment: She slept in the beautiful bedroom, in the comfortable bed, and admired the green satin drapes before she fell asleep.

Herman opened up the couch in the living room and went to bed. But he could not sleep. Two people are sleeping in the next room . . . one not yet born. My wife and my child! he thought. He had called his parents in Arecibo and they had spoken to Alice; their joy was as great as his. Yes, I have my own family, he said, and his eyes filled with tears.

At last he could think about his own parents and feel right, not ashamed of his feelings. An inner peace filled him and he drifted into a deep, tranquil sleep.

Kique's birth was normal and Alice was able to be on her feet and walking the next day. When they brought the baby in to her, she was amazed. It didn't seem possible that this perfect tiny person had come from inside her. The baby had lots of soft, light-brown hair and a pinkish complexion. He's real light-skinned, thought Alice; just like Stevie. For a moment she felt depressed. She did not want to remember Stevie. Herman is kinda light-skinned and he got brown hair, Alice reasoned as she held the baby, feeling all right again.

She looked at Kique as he sucked away contentedly at his bottle, and the pain of childbirth seemed far away. During labor, Alice had promised herself that she would never again endure such pain. She had screamed at the top of her lungs, and had blamed her mother for not warning her about such agony. But now as she looked at Kique, she just could not imagine life without him. He's just so beautiful, she thought, holding him tightly and feeling warm and happy all over.

The baby was named after Herman's father, Enrique Alfonso Aviles, and called Kique for short. Herman had cabled his family in Arecibo, giving them the baby's weight and height and all the details. Herman had managed to have all the necessary equipment ready as he waited for Kique's arrival.

Part III

Life changed radically for Alice. Kique cried every morning at 2 A.M. and had to be fed and walked until he fell asleep. Sometimes this took several hours. Herman would get up and relieve her part of the time, so that she could go back to bed. He left early in the morning for work, and Alice had to start all over again. During the day she had to do the housework and manage all alone. At first her mother came and helped out, but as time went by, her visits became few and brief. "I have my own family, Alice, and I have to go to work. You gonna have to manage the best way you can, just like everybody else. Of course, in an emergency . . ." Alice had shrugged her shoulders; she had never counted very much on her mother anyway. Luis is all that matters to her, she had told herself.

Since she had no friends, Alice spent most of her time alone in the apartment. It was still winter and cold out, so she could not take the baby for walks. Except for the visits to the doctor for checkups, Alice's world was the apartment.

The days were long for Alice, and she watched the clock with desperation, waiting for the evening when Herman would walk through the door. He helped her with the household chores, and devoted the rest of his time to Kique. Kique was growing into a fine healthy boy. Alice never objected to what Herman said, nor did she complain about being tired or lonely.

Things are going well, Herman thought.

146

At night, alone in bed, Alice remembered about Herman and what she knew. After all, he had told her how it was, she thought. It seemed that all he really cared about was the baby.

Alice opened the kitchen window and looked out. People had shed their winter clothing and the days were getting lighter and longer. She smiled. Spring is really here! A sun-shower had left everything wet and shiny. Alice inhaled the sweet, damp, warm air. She had started to take Kique out for walks. The neighbors were all friendly, accepting her and Herman, often commenting about the baby. Several of the women had complimented the baby's good looks. ". . . Exactly like his father; he's going to grow up to look distinguished. There is definitely a strong resemblance to Mr. Aviles." Alice had responded by saying that he looked even more like his grandfather in Arecibo, Puerto Rico. ". . . He's even named after him too," she had said proudly.

She stepped away from the window, glancing at the clock on the wall. Olga will be here soon, she said to herself. These past few days, as she walked with Kique she had met some of the kids she knew. They were coming home from school. She had been especially pleased when she met Olga Fuentes. Olga had walked along with Alice, telling her classmates to go on ahead. For several days now, Alice and Olga had met and walked together. She invited her friend to come up and visit after school.

"I got some good coffee cake Herman brings from work; we can have some. Come on over tomorrow after school, O.K.?"

Olga accepted, and Alice made sure the house was neat and everything was in order. Her heart beat fast as she thought of her visitor. She had not seen any of her friends for so long. Now, as the excitement mounted, she hoped she wouldn't say anything too silly. The baby was napping. Alice had the radio on softly; they were playing a popular love ballad. The doorbell rang. Quickly, she turned off the radio and opened the door. Olga smiled at her.

"Hi, Alice, I'm here."

"Hi, Olga, come on in."

Olga walked in and held up her schoolbooks. "Where can I put these?" she asked.

"Give me them; I'll put them here on the kitchen cabinet. Come on in, Olga. You never been here—let me show you the house."

Olga followed Alice from the kitchen into the living room.

"Man, this is really nice," Olga said, impressed. "You sure got a lotta nice things here."

"Thanks. Yeah, Herman likes to have good things. He is always picking up something for the house."

"Where is Kique?" asked Olga.

"He's napping. I put him in his crib to nap early today. That way, we can talk."

"Can I see him? Please, Alice, I wanted to see him."

"You'll see him. Come on into the bedroom, but don't make no noise. He'll be up soon enough." They tiptoed over to the crib where Kique slept soundly, sucking a pacifier.

"What a little doll," Olga whispered softly. They walked back to the living room. "That's some sharp bedroom set you got, Alice. I love them drapes and spread."

148

"Yeah, it's beautiful. Herman bought it."

"He sure got some sharp taste."

"That he does," agreed Alice. "Do you know him? Did you ever meet him?"

"I never met him personally. But I seen him, you know . . . walking around. He's very distinguished-looking."

"You gotta come some evening and meet him. He's really nice."

"Really?" Olga asked, impressed.

"Yeah, I mean it. You'll like him. He's not at all stuck up or nothing."

"O.K." Olga nodded.

"Come on and have some of that cake I told you about."

The two girls went into the kitchen and Alice set out some cake and milk. They began to eat silently. After a while, Alice asked, "How's school, Olga?"

"Good. You know, the same. Mrs. Rudolf is still reporting everybody for talking . . . and you know the gym teacher, Miss MacIntosh? Well, she quit. Can you imagine? You'll never guess, man: She got married!"

"Married?"

"Yeah, right? Everybody said she was queer. . . . Like she pinches the girls and all. But—" Olga shrugged her shoulders. "—she quit to get married and she's gonna live in another state. You know what? . . . Remember those two sisters, Tessie and Marie? Well, you know that boy, Robert . . . real tall? They said that they like him, and that . . ."

Alice listened with great interest as Olga went on talking about school, the teachers, and her friends. Alice surprised herself; she had not been aware of the many things she wanted to know.

"This is a really nice place," Olga said. Alice nodded. "You know, I didn't even know you got married. I didn't know you knew him, even. Your husband, I mean. You never told me."

"Well," Alice said, looking away, "it was just one of them things. We got married right after Christmas."

"I'm glad for you, Alice. Really, I know you must be happy. My mother said you are lucky to have such a nice husband." Alice looked at Olga but remained silent. After a while she realized that Olga was staring at her, waiting for a response.

"He is a very nice man," she said. Her voice was very low.

They heard a cry coming from the bedroom. Alice jumped up.

"It's Kique—he woke up already. What did I tell you?"

"Oh, good," Olga said. "Now I can play with him."

The two girls went into the bedroom.

"Alice, why don't you come to my birthday party? You know, I'm gonna be sixteen. It's my sweet-sixteen party. Hey! Alice, man, I forgot, you are gonna be sixteen too. Right? My birthday is just before yours."

"Yours is the tenth and mine is the twenty-first," said Alice.

"Why don't you come? We are gonna have a ball. I'm inviting a lot of the kids from the school and some of my cousins are also coming from Manhattan. Come on, will you?"

"I'll feel stupid," Alice said.

"Go on, why? You'll know practically everybody there."

"I don't know. . . . I . . . I don't think so." Alice shook her head.

"Why not? Bring your husband and bring Kique too. O.K.?"

"Well," Alice said, "I don't know if it's such a good idea. Kique gets cranky sometimes, and he—"

"We'll all play with him. He's so cute," Olga interrupted. "Look—if he gets sleepy, he can go to sleep in one of the bedrooms. Come on, please? Will you?"

"I'll ask Herman," Alice said, smiling.

"Good!" Olga jumped up with joy. "Now it's settled."

"What about your mother, Olga?"

"She won't mind—why should she?"

"She did mind before though, didn't she?"

"Listen, that was before you—you know . . ." Olga responded. "But you got married and everything. She knows I'm visiting you right now, and she don't mind at all. She asks me how you and the baby are. I swear, Alice, honest."

"We'll see." Alice shrugged, smiling with pleasure. "Too bad you gotta leave. Listen, come back again any time. Any time at all. You don't have to ask. Like if you just feel like dropping over, come by. And if you don't see me downstairs after school, then you can go home first and then come here."

"I had a really great time, Alice. Thanks. Maybe I'll come by tomorrow."

"Good, and also come later in the evening too and you can meet Herman. He knows all about you—I already told him. O.K.?"

"Swell. And don't forget to ask him about my party?"

They said good-bye and Olga left. Alice could not put the idea of the party out of her mind. Man, I'll wear a sharp dress now that I got my figure back, she said to herself, and

151

giggled out loud. I wonder who is gonna be there? She had seen many of the kids she knew coming out of school these past few weeks. When they greeted each other, Alice felt like an outsider. Now the party made her feel different. An excitement took over, and she felt a surge of boundless energy.

She began to jump around, dancing and throwing her arms about. Kique watched from his playpen and shrieked, wanting to be picked up. Alice stopped moving and looked at Kique. She didn't want to pick him up; she didn't want to play with him or look at him.

Alice awoke, stretched, yawned, and shut her eyes again. She remembered the party last night and felt good. Man, what a ball! That was some great party, she said to herself. She had danced and danced; laughed so hard. She knew just about everybody who was there. Like everybody was so nice and friendly. She smiled as she remembered. Like old times —only better because Frankie had asked her to dance over and over again. Alice opened her eyes and glanced at the clock on the night table. It was still early. Kique slept soundly in his crib. She closed her eyes, hoping that Kique would let her sleep a little longer. When Herman had decided not to go to the party, she had been relieved. He had insisted she go by herself, and Alice had been overjoyed.

The music was fabulous, and Olga had all the latest records. The kids were great. They taught her all the new dance steps. At first the boys were shy with her, and she felt awkward. But after a while everybody was kidding around, just like old times. She thought about how she felt each time that Frankie asked her to dance. She had known

Frankie López from way back. He never gave me a tumble, she thought, and like now, wow! . . . Her mind seemed to be swimming, and her body felt weak and limp. It had been a long time since she had felt this way about anybody. When could she see Frankie again, she wondered. If she did . . . what would he say? or do? What will I say to him? she asked herself.

Alice curled up happily, pulling the covers tightly around her. She couldn't wait to see Olga and find out what Frankie had said . . . what everybody had said about her. She was dying to talk to Olga.

Herman lit a cigarette. He was in bed feeling restless. Annoyed, he thought about Olga. He resented her constant visits. They were always whispering and giggling, and Alice always became so silly when she was with Olga. Lately, he had tried to accept her, realizing that she was Alice's only friend. He had told her that he was uncomfortable at parties, and that he did not dance.

"Go on ahead, Alice, have a good time. You hardly ever go out. I'll stay with Kique."

He had not expected her to come home so late. Maybe I should have gone—after all, I am her husband. Herman smiled, feeling ridiculous. When he thought about Kique, these feelings passed quickly; the baby mattered very much to him. What was more difficult for Herman was getting Daniel out of his mind. Very often he would imagine meeting Daniel, quite accidentally, and talking to him, trying to explain about Alice and Kique. He would have to make him understand that there was nothing between him and the girl. It was the baby that mattered; Kique needed him. Nothing had gone on at all; he had been faithful. It was silly to go on like this, he would say to himself. Once he thought he actually saw him, and his heart seemed to stop for an instant. The sense of relief when he saw that the young man was not Daniel was not nearly as great as his disappointment. Herman asked himself, If he came back to me, could I say no? What about Kique? What will Daniel say to me? Herman went into the kitchen to fix Kique's bottle. I'll feed him this morning, he said to himself. Alice is probably too tired to wake up.

It was warm and humid out. Herman sat in the living room with the windows wide open. He was not really listening to the television program he watched. Where the hell is she? he thought. He went into the kitchen and glanced at the clock on the wall. Almost midnight. He poured himself a glass of cold juice. Every night it's the same thing. Off she goes with Olga and she's not back till midnight, he said to himself. Who does she think I am? Who does she think she is, anyway? She forgets where she was until I gave her a home. "I'm not putting up with this crap," Herman mumbled out loud. Several times he had tried to speak to Alice, but she had rushed into the bedroom. Last night he had knocked on the bedroom door, but she had not answered. Herman sipped his cold juice, feeling better. Yes, tonight; tonight she'll talk to me. Herman heard the front door and quickly jumped up. Alice tried to walk past him to the bedroom. He put out his right arm, blocking the way.

"Well?" He looked at her. Alice did not answer—she stared at him silently. "Where were you, Alice? It's very late."

"Around," she answered, her voice very low. It was the first time he had confronted her. She felt herself shaking.

"Around where?" his voice was loud and clear.

"Around with Olga . . . just around. . . ."

"Just around? Don't you think you can manage to stay home one evening? This is every night with Olga!"

"She's my friend. I didn't think you was gonna mind!"

"Well, I do! I do mind!" Herman shouted. "This is not a hotel."

"What should I do instead? Get a pass from you, teacher?"

"What do you mean by that, Alice?"

"I—I mean what's the difference? Supper is made and Kique is ready for bed. You don't gotta do nothing. Why should I be here? I don't do nothing all day anyway, except take care of this place!"

"You live here, don't you? This is your home, too! You forget easily, don't you? Remember how I found you? How you were? Do you remember?"

"All right!" Alice said loudly. "Thanks. Thank you very much. O.K.? Satisfied? Is that all? May I go now?"

Herman did not know what to say. Alice turned away and started toward the bedroom once again.

"Wait, Alice. We have to straighten this thing out. We made an agreement and should . . ."

"I take care of the house, right?" Alice interrupted.

"And I pay for everything, damn it! I work for you and Kique, don't I?" Herman could not control his anger, and shouted, "How do you think we live?"

"I said thanks! Thank you!"

155

"Alice!" Herman shouted. "That's enough!"

"Look, Herman." Alice's voice was unsteady. "I'm not staying home, Herman. No more, I'm not." She shook her head. "No," she whispered.

"You have responsibilities, Alice."

"What responsibilities? I do my job. I don't interfere with you. Leave my life alone!"

"What do you mean, leave your life alone? What do you think I am? Where do you think you live? What about Kique?"

"What about Kique?" Alice screamed. "He's your son now, ain't he? That's all you wanted—to get a son. Now leave me alone, you hear? You leave me alone, and I'll leave you alone."

"As long as I head this house, I have a right . . . a right to demand to know when you go out and when you come home. As Kique's mother you have to be part of this family."

"I'm not staying home, Herman. I'm going out when I please, and when I want to."

"And the baby?" interrupted Herman. "What about him?"

"What about him?" Alice asked. "You don't think I'm good enough for my baby? Good, go get another one. You want a baby, Herman? Go make one. . . . Go ahead, I dare you, go make a baby!" she shrieked. "I'm sick of you and I'm tired of this whole mess. What family? I'm doing what I want, when I want, with who I want!"

"You bitch." Herman's voice was almost inaudible with anger. He went toward Alice, who ducked his blows, running into the bedroom, slamming the door. "You filthy little tramp. . . . I ought to—" He pushed the door, feeling Alice's weight against it. Stopping abruptly, he went back into the living room.

"Fag! Bastard! You old fairy!" Alice whispered. When she realized he had left, she sat on the bed and covered her face with her hands, crying. After a while she checked Kique, who slept soundly, sucking his pacifier.

Alice sighed, wishing Frankie were here with her. She saw him every night. She could not bear the thought of being away from him even for one night. Except for Kique, she knew she loved him better than anyone in the whole world. She was tired of hiding from Frankie's parents and from Herman. No more, she said to herself. I'm not gonna hide from nobody. I'm gonna put it to Frankie like it is. We can live together; we could get a place and he can get a job. He was quitting school, and they planned to get their own place instead of always meeting in somebody's house. Thank God for Olga, she thought. She's gonna be my maid of honor when Frankie and me get married, Alice said to herself, pleased.

"I hate Herman. I hate him!" she whispered out loud.

Alice undressed and went to bed. She felt less angry at Herman and sorry about what she had said to him. Well, I guess I did make him angry, she thought. Maybe when I tell him about Frankie, he'll understand. Anyway, I gotta tell him. Maybe I'll tell him tomorrow."

Herman puffed on his cigarette in the dark. He could not fall asleep. At first he was livid with anger, but now he felt helpless. She's right, he said to himself, almost laughing.

What family? What household? His attachment to Kique was all that really mattered, after all. It can't last, you know, he said to himself; nothing ever lasts for me. She's more honest than I am. As he thought of Kique, his love for the baby was shaken. He's her child. . . . Kique is hers. He felt uneasy. She's going to leave and she's taking the baby. But it doesn't really matter. If she doesn't go I'll kick her out. God, what a mess. I wonder who she's seeing? Some other kid like herself. Making babies. Lots of unwanted babies.

Herman thought about his parents and felt a need to be near them. To see them once again. It's time to leave . . . leave this neighborhood and leave New York. Herman put out his cigarette. Maybe, he said to himself, I should see about a job in San Juan. I might get back to Puerto Rico after all.

Part IV

Herman carefully packed things away. The movers were due at noon. Everything was going into storage. At nine thirty tomorrow he was taking the plane to Puerto Rico. His family would meet him at the airport in San Juan, and then they would all drive to Arecibo. He had planned everything carefully, and was pleased as always that things were going on schedule.

Herman put all of Kique's pictures into a small photo album, which he packed into his suitcase. The breakup had been painless, almost matter-of-fact. He had wished Alice lots of luck and hoped that she and Frankie would be happy.

158

She could file for an annulment or divorce on any grounds—he would not protest. She, in turn, promised to keep him informed about Kique.

The first few weeks were hard. Herman missed the baby and the routine, but very soon he got used to living alone again. Four months had passed since he had heard from Alice. The last time, she had sent him a small photograph of Kique. At the beginning, Herman was almost tempted to visit them just to see the baby, but was glad he hadn't. He had written her a letter this morning including some money for Kique. The other letter in his pocket was for Daniel. He was sending it to his old address and hoped it would be forwarded.

He wondered about his job interview next week in San Juan. I hope I get the position, he said to himself. Looking around at the apartment, he thought, In any event, I won't ever come back here.

Herman continued to pack. I wonder when these moving guys are going to get here. They are late. Herman laughed at himself as he realized he was mumbling out loud again.

Alice saw the nurse coming toward her. She was groggy from all the medication and injections they had given her. The pain was still unbearable, and she moaned in protest. The large nurse approached her, smiling, and wiped her head with a cool washcloth.

"There, there, little mother. Now, no screaming. You must be quiet. Shh!" She put her forefinger up to her mouth and smiled. "Now, the doctor will be here very, very soon. Hold on. Be nice and quiet, or else the baby will refuse to come out if he hears all that yelling." The nurse turned and left.

Alice wanted to speak, but it took all the strength she had just to bear the pain. She felt her face and body wet with perspiration. She wanted to scream out to the nurse to come back and tell her how long she had been in labor. Was it hours? Or days? . . . she wondered. Her head was spinning. She had been through this before, long ago. Alice kept drifting away into a dreamlike state. She saw the apartment—it was so real. How nice everything was, and she was waiting for Herman. Yes . . . there he is, smiling at her. Oh, look, he brought her something. She wanted to take it from him, but he disappeared. Alice felt the pain again. She had left the apartment a long time ago. God, yes, with Frankie. Yeah, of course, Frankie. What was she doing here now? She was no longer with Frankie, that's right. She and Frankie had split up. Now she remembered! That no-good bum, leaving her and Kique, walking out, and she didn't even have a cent. She never wanted to see him again. Wait then . . . Alice was drifting and drifting. . . . Here's Herman. He's asking me something. What? What is it?

"Alice do you want anything? I can pick it up on my way home from work."

She felt herself spinning. The pain was unbearable. Where was the nurse? Somebody should help her—tell her—where she was. Where was she and who was she with? It's not Frankie. What happened? Who was she with now? She couldn't remember. Alice felt herself burning up; her hands were wet and sticky. I have to remember. I am having a baby . . . yes, that's right. She felt better. O.K., but who am

160

I with now? Dear God! Alice began to panic. She had to get out of here and find out what this was all about! The pain was getting worse and worse. . . . Luis. I remember, Luis's cousin. Yes, Albert, that's his name. Thank God. . . . Alice began to pray. . . . Please, I mustn't forget his name. . . .

"Nurse, nurse . . . quick! Hurry up, this patient is ready. Let's go—the baby is coming down. Hurry! Hurry! . . ." Alice heard the doctor shouting at the nurse and felt herself being placed on a stretcher and wheeled into another room.

She stared at the ceiling, bright lights that almost blinded her. Someone put a mask on her face.

"Breathe deeply now. . . breathe," a voice said. Alice felt herself drifting and drifting. . . .

How nice everything looked. He was smiling at her.

"Herman? Would you like to feel the baby? It's moving again." Herman moved over and, sitting close to Alice, put his hands on her stomach.

"Ave María! . . . You got an acrobat inside there, Alice, I swear," Herman said, laughing.

She was very, very happy.

LOVE WITH ALELUYA

"There she goes, Joey. Go on!" Hannibal said, and gave Joey a slight shove. Joey did not move as he watched Serafina coming toward them. "Will you go on? We only got a couple of minutes between classes, man!" Hannibal urged. "The bell's gonna ring."

"All right . . . O.K., just a minute!" Joey whispered.

His eyes met hers as she walked by. Serafina fluttered her long dark lashes and, tilting her head back, looked away from Joey. Before Hannibal could say another word, Joey followed Serafina down the school corridor. Walking beside her, he could feel his cheeks burning.

Her perfect posture and straight back accentuated her full breasts, which were clearly silhouetted under her sweater. Serafina's long black hair hung loosely down her back, just above her tiny waist. Joey watched as she swung her hips from side to side, walking at a quick pace. Clearing his throat, he said, "Hi," and smiled. Serafina continued to walk, looking straight ahead. "You're beautiful, baby, you know that? Huh, Mami?" And pursing his lips together, he bent over and made a kissing sound in her ear. She tilted her head back and heaved a sigh. Joey looked at her bosom once more and said, "Do that again." Serafina turned and walked into a classroom. " 'Bye, beautiful. You gonna give me a heart attack, baby, looking and acting like that," he called after her.

"Well, did you ask her out?" Hannibal asked.

"She don't even talk to me; how am I gonna ask her out?" Joey answered.

"What you been doing all this time, man? It's been days now you have been following that chick around. All you have to do is ask."

"Just like that, huh? You think it's so easy?" Joey said, annoyed. A bell sounded.

"Come on, we're late," Hannibal said, and Joey followed him.

After school, Joey and Hannibal waited outside by the side exit they knew Serafina used.

"They gonna be with her again, man, I know it!" Joey said with exasperation.

"Maybe not, Joey. Let's just wait and see," Hannibal said.

The Morris High School schoolyard was crowded with students, some talking and others coming or going. Their friends and classmates waved to the two boys.

"Hi, man. How you doing?"

"What's happening, baby?"

"Que pasa, man?"

Hannibal and Joey waved and answered.

"Fine . . . everything's cool."

"We doing just great. . . ."

The two boys waited patiently. Finally the door opened

163

and a boy of about sixteen walked out, followed by Serafina and another boy who was taller and older. She did not look in Joey's direction. All three passed by silently and walked down the street out of sight.

"See that?" Joey threw up his hands. "They come up to the classroom to get her, yet. . . . She can't go nowhere without her brothers chaperoning her all the time. Man, like she's gonna disappear or something."

"Well, of all the good-looking chicks around, you had to pick a greenhorn," Hannibal said, "and one that belongs to that Aleluya church as well." He shook his head.

Joey shrugged his shoulders. "Well, you gotta admit, she's something else!"

"That's your problem, not mine. I'm not the one stuck on her."

"Aww . . . man, Hannibal. Come on! How many times I helped you out? If that's the way you gonna be—"

"All right," Hannibal interrupted. "You know I'm gonna help you. We'll think of something, don't worry." Hannibal extended his hand toward Joey. "You my man, Joey, my main man!"

Joey smiled and, raising his hand, brought it down, slapping Hannibal's open palm.

"All right!" he said.

The two boys started home.

"Look—there's Ramona, Mary, and Casilda," Joey said.

"Hey, Joey, maybe they know something about Serafina," Hannibal whispered.

"Come on, Hannibal, I don't want everybody to know that I like her."

164

"Wait a minute," Hannibal said. "I'll ask. You just let me do the talking, O.K.? You don't say nothing."

"O.K., Hannibal, but remember—"

"Shh," Hannibal said. "Just be quiet."

They walked alongside the three girls.

"Hi, how you doing?" Hannibal said.

"Oh," Ramona said. "Hi, Hannibal." They all exchanged greetings.

"Hey, any of you girls know that new girl from Puerto Rico?"

"What girl?" asked Mary.

"You know her. She's got a real thick accent—she's only been here since the beginning of term, last September. She's got real long hair," Hannibal said.

"Oh, yeah—Serafina. That's who you mean?" asked Ramona. "Why?"

"Yeah, her. I was just wondering if you are friends with her."

"Are you kidding? Friends with her?" Ramona laughed. "First of all, she's older than us. I heard she's almost eighteen. And second, she can hardly speak English. She got a real thick accent. Anyway, she's such a greenhorn—"

"Yeah," interrupted Casilda, "and she's not Catholic, so we don't even see that girl in church. She belongs to that Pentecostal church, the one on Prospect Avenue near Westchester."

"Those people of that religion are very strict," said Mary. "I don't know that they would let her be friends with us. Like—her brothers are always walking with her somewhere. I never seen her alone. She's always with another girl or somebody, never by herself in the street, never."

"Why are you so interested in her, Hannibal?" Ramona said, smiling. Mary and Casilda began to giggle.

"Just asking," Hannibal replied, shrugging his shoulders.

"Oh . . ." said Ramona. "Just asking?" She looked at her two friends. "You must like her accent." All three girls laughed out loud.

Joey felt himself blushing and looked at Hannibal.

"You funny, you know that?" Hannibal said to Ramona. "Come on, Joey, let's get out of here."

They turned and crossed the street.

"Brush up on your Spanish, Hannibal," Ramona called out.

"Do your exercises, flat chest!" Hannibal replied loudly. "I seen grapes bigger than what you got. . . ."

"Shhh," Joey said. "See what you done? Now you got everybody curious."

"So what! They think *I* like her, not you, so you got nothing to worry about."

"Well," said Joey. "But we didn't get anywhere."

"O.K., then we gotta make some plans. That's all."

"What plans?" asked Joey.

"We are gonna take a look at that church," Hannibal replied.

"What?"

"Just listen to your boy," Hannibal said. Joey shrugged his shoulders and followed Hannibal, waiting to hear his plans.

That Friday evening, Hannibal and Joey stood on the corner of Prospect Avenue, looking toward the storefront

166

church. A hand-printed sign was boldly placed on the large window. It read:

LA SALVACION DE ADAM Y EVA
Iglesia Pentecostal del Bronx, Inc.

Underneath, a mural depicted a large yellow brick wall, with the top of an apple tree visible and in full bloom. Large red apples were more abundant than green leaves. In front of the wall, a large white cross outlined in gold and emitting golden rays dominated the scene. In a corner, a dead green rattlesnake was covered with bright orange blood.

The two boys watched as groups of people filed into the church carrying small black Bibles. They saw Serafina, her parents, and her two brothers enter the church.

"When do you think Ralphy and Perry are gonna get here?" Joey asked.

"We told them at eight o'clock, so let's wait awhile."

After a few moments, they heard a shrill whistle and saw Ralphy and Perry walking toward them.

"How we doing?" asked Perry.

"They are almost ready to start, I think. Let's wait till we see them close the door. Then we can go over and investigate the scene," said Hannibal.

"Man, I hope this whole thing is worth it, Hannibal," said Perry. "I ain't been inside one of them places since I was a little kid, and I got caught yelling. They chased my tail out, and I ran like crazy."

"Come on now, we got nothing to lose, and at the same time we help out our boy," Hannibal said, winking at Joey.

167

Joey blushed and looked away. "They got some fine-looking chicks in there, man," Hannibal went on, "and when they have their attacks, everybody gets the holy spirit. And the girls throw themselves on anybody who's there to catch them. That will be us. Joey will catch Serafina, and we will have our own choice; we just look around and see who we all like."

"Maybe they'll throw us out, like they did to Perry," said Ralphy.

"Not if we behave ourselves and come in like gentlemens. We just sit in the back and say we are curious, that's all. You see, they are always looking for someone to save. My aunt was in that kinda church when I was a kid, and I used to go with her a lot. We'll just act like we are interested in getting saved. But cool now, real cool. Just sort of curious, you know, let them think they can save us, and man—we will be in good with them people. And our boy here"—Hannibal paused and pointed to Joey—"can get in real good with Serafina and her brothers and all."

"What do you think?" Ralphy asked, looking at Perry. Perry shrugged his shoulders.

"Aww, man," Hannibal said, "I thought we agreed. You guys are not gonna chicken out now, are you?"

"O.K.," Perry said. "But . . . look, if it gets too messy, we split. O.K.?"

"All right," Hannibal answered, "you got a deal. And you won't be sorry. Wait till you see some of them chicks. Ave María . . ." Hannibal made the sign of the cross. "Especially the jibaritas. Them greenhorn babies are built. . . . Umm—what bodies! And man, they can't hardly speak no

168

English. They'll be at our mercy. And I'm ready to save them all." Hannibal smiled broadly and pointed to himself. "I am the Savior, aleluya." The boys laughed as they watched Hannibal spread out his arms. "Come here, Mami—Papi is ready to save you." He looked at his captured audience and after a while continued in a more serious tone. "O.K., we ready now, but no laughing in there. We are all gonna be caballeros."

The boys walked up to the church. The door was shut, but they could hear the minister's voice preaching his sermon. Carefully, Hannibal looked through the large storefront window, finding areas where there was no paint and the glass was clear.

"Look," he whispered, "there's Serafina—over there. . . . And she's sitting with a bunch of girls near the back."

"Where?" asked Joey. Motioning and pointing, Hannibal showed his friends where Serafina and the girls were sitting.

"O.K.," Hannibal said. "Now, I'm gonna go in. Just follow me; we sit right in back of them. There are some empty seats. You, Joey, try to sit directly in back of Serafina. Let's go!" Hannibal waited a moment and then opened the door. As they entered, they heard the minister's voice.

"Our Lord is powerful and mighty; He loves his children but demands commitment. . . ." He stopped preaching as the boys walked in and closed the door behind them. Hannibal led them to the row behind Serafina. All four squeezed in, forcing the people to move over and leave them enough room to sit. The minister pushed his glasses down toward the tip of his nose and peered at the visitors. People turned in their seats looking at the boys, and a soft whispering

169

sounded among the congregation. ". . . total commitment," the minister went on. "El Señor is jealous of His children's love. He works in mysterious ways, and sends us souls when we least expect them." He cleared his throat. "We will prove to Him our faith and commitment tonight. Let us reach out so that He may touch us! Purify us! Free us of our sins!"

"Aleluya."

"Amen. Jesucristo!"

"Save us. Aleluya!"

People shouted and responded as the minister spoke.

Joey moved into the seat directly in back of Serafina and next to Hannibal.

"Her family is over there," Hannibal whispered into Joey's ear. Joey nodded nervously.

"Yes, sir!" the minister continued. "Tonight. Yes, indeed! Reach out . . . let Him touch us all. Don't be afraid. The Lord our Master loves you, wants you."

People shouted, and some began to stand and sway.

"El Señor will save us with His love."

"Sinners! We are all no-good sinners."

A woman stepped into the center aisle and began to speak loudly in tongues.

"Sha . . . bala . . . cucha mon la dabah . . . shandala la . . . la . . . wa shon . . ." She waved her arms frantically. Everyone encouraged her as she moaned and continued to speak. Others began to shriek.

"Up here . . . here," the minister shouted. "Show the new-comers to the house of God. Show them what can be done with faith."

"What's the matter with that lady?" asked Ralphy. "What kinda language is she talking?"

170

"She's got the spirit, and she's talking in tongues. That's a language they use when they are talking to God."

"Man," Ralphy said, and shook his head in disbelief.

"Wait, man," Hannibal said. "They all gonna get the spirit. Wait." He gestured to the girls in front of them.

Serafina turned briefly and stared at Joey. Then she turned back, once more looking straight ahead.

"Hey, Joey," Hannibal whispered. "Do something, man."

"What?"

"Give her a little feel, man," Hannibal said softly. Joey did not answer, and Hannibal dug his elbow into Joey's arm.

The musicians began to play the piano, guitar, violin, and drums. Several people held tambourines and accompanied the musicians. The congregation was busy clapping, shouting, jumping, moving, and dancing to the music. Everyone seemed caught up in the excitement of the music and the shouts of joy.

"Let her know you are here, will you?" Hannibal insisted, and looked at Joey with exasperation.

Joey glanced around to make sure that no one was looking at them, and sitting forward apprehensively, he slipped his arm through the opening in the back of her chair, caressing Serafina's rib cage. She jumped up in her seat, but did not turn around. The other girls turned around and, looking at the boys, whispered among themselves quietly, giggling.

Leaning forward, Hannibal said to the girl in front of him, "Hi, how are you doing, beautiful? What's your name? You know, you remind me of a movie star. I swear, baby." The girl did not respond. Smiling, he tapped Perry and Ralphy, motioning to them that they should speak to the girls. Both boys were busy looking at the congregation and the musicians. They ignored Hannibal as he tried unsuccessfully to get them interested.

All of a sudden, the music stopped and everyone was quiet. The minister was in front of the pulpit on the platform. He held out his arms, towering over the people who stood before him.

"I will touch you, and through me you will feel the Lord." As he touched them, they fell to their knees limply and help-lessly. Shouts of praise sounded from the congregation.

"Praise be to God!"

"Have mercy, oh Lord!"

The minister continued to pray and touch whoever came up to the pulpit.

"How about the newcomers?" the minister shouted. "Will they come up here and let the Lord touch them?" He looked in their direction. "Will you come up here, young men?"

"I'm splitting, man," Perry said. "This is too much for me." Ralphy nodded in agreement. As they started to stand, they heard a piercing scream which filled the church. Serafina was standing, shrieking and waving her arms.

"Eeeeeeee . . . ayyyyy . . ."

Another girl stood up and began to moan and sway.

"Let's cut," Ralphy said, standing. Perry followed.

"Wait a minute," said Hannibal. "Let's see."

"You wait a minute, Hannibal," said Perry.

"But, listen—" protested Hannibal.

"Listen, you save them," said Ralphy. "You their savior, ain't you? Not me, man; this here is too wild." Both boys walked out into the aisle and swiftly left the church.

Hannibal and Joey sat still as they watched Serafina and

two other girls shriek and moan while being escorted by several men up to the minister. He began to pray over them.

"Well?" Joey said, looking anxiously at Hannibal.

"You shoulda grabbed her, Joey," he said.

"What? I didn't see you grab nobody."

"Of course not," said Hannibal. "I was waiting for you to grab Serafina first."

"And what was I supposed to do with her while everybody here is looking?"

"Man, Joey." Hannibal shook his head and sighed. "You could just be helpful and try to be friendly, that's all."

"Aww, man, Hannibal," Joey said, annoyed.

"We might as well go ourselves. Like there's nothing we gonna do now. What you say, Joey?"

"Right you are," Joey agreed quickly.

Everyone was shouting and screaming. No one seemed to take notice of them. They walked out slowly to the center aisle, stopping as they looked toward the front at Serafina and the two girls, who were now clapping and jumping along with a group of people.

"Aleluya, the Lord be praised," shouted the minister. "Here come our two young brothers."

In an instant, Hannibal felt himself being quickly escorted to the pulpit. A man on each side held him by his elbows so forcefully that his feet seemed to leave the ground.

Joey followed as two men escorted him in a similar manner.

With arms outstretched, looking down at both boys, the minister smiled. The thick lenses of his eyeglasses made his eyes look larger than they actually were. He waved his arms gracefully, as if he were conducting a chorus. The church was quiet.

"Almighty God. Thank you for sending us these young souls." Looking down at Joey and Hannibal, he asked, "Do you want to be saved?" Not waiting for a response, he continued, "Oh yes, Lord, they want to be saved . . . and that's why they came up here. Aleluya!"

"Aleluya."

"Praise the Lord. . . . Glory to God!"

People called out, and some sobbed loudly.

Joey and Hannibal stood perfectly still.

"Confess! Confess to Jesus. Feel free, my sons. Jesus wants you to be free." Stepping down from the platform, the minister stood before Hannibal.

"What's your name, son?" he asked Hannibal. "Let Jesus, Our Lord, and everyone here know your name. Amen."

"Hannibal . . . Soto."

"Do you want to feel the Lord? Do you want him to touch you?"

Hannibal sighed. He managed to turn and saw that everyone was staring at him. He looked at Joey, who appeared to be in pain. Hannibal cleared his throat, trying not to make a sound.

"Don't be afraid, my son." The minister smiled, tilting his back and looking at the ceiling. "The Lord is with us."

He stepped over to Joey and repeated what he had said to Hannibal. Joey kept smiling and nodding timidly at everything the minister said.

Backing away from the boys, he signaled to the musicians. They began to play softly. The music was a slow waltz with a sharp drumbeat. People began to sway and hum.

"Oh, Lord, here we have two boys. Help us reach them. Help them, sweet Jesus, to open up. Gather them into your hearts, touch them, free them!"

Quickly, he went over and touched Hannibal on the head and shoulders. Without any thought of disobeying, Hannibal fell down to his knees. As the minister touched Joey, he did exactly as Hannibal.

"Oh, Lord. Thank you! Thank you! You have given us two souls and now they are yours, sweet Jesus."

And as the minister spoke, Hannibal silently prayed that Ralphy and Perry were not looking in through the storefront window.

The following Monday at school, as Joey and Hannibal walked along the corridor, they saw Serafina. To their surprise, she walked up to them.

"Hello," she said.

"Hi," said Joey.

"How are you doing?" said Hannibal.

"Did you enjoy the services?" she smiled. They both nodded, feeling uncomfortable.

Joey glanced at her formfitting sweater and full hips and felt the blood rushing all over his body.

"How about we see each other?" he asked.

"Today," she said, "after school, yes, sí? Outside, in the side entrance." The bell sounded, and she rushed off down the corridor.

"How about that?" said Hannibal. "See? You got it made. What did I tell you; now you are in good with her."

Joey smiled at Hannibal, trying not to blush.

"Come with me, O.K., Hannibal?"

"Sure," he said. "Maybe she got a friend."

Hannibal and Joey waited by the side entrance after school.

"Do you think she'll come alone, Hannibal? You know, without no escorts?"

"Sure. Man, Joey, did you see the way she looked at you? Aleluya is right! She looks like she got the spirit, all right. And you gonna save her."

Joey laughed nervously, shifting his weight from side to side and looking at the entrance.

The boys greeted their friends as they passed by, and continued to wait. A few moments later, the door opened and Serafina appeared, followed by her two brothers. All three walked up to the boys.

The older brother extended his hand toward Hannibal, and then toward Joey.

"Juan Martínez de la Cruz," he said shaking hands.

The younger brother did the same, saying, "Josefo Martínez de la Cruz."

"We want you to have these," Juan said, and handed each boy a small black Bible. "God will be with you and accompany you every moment of the day and night. Amen . . . Aleluya."

Hannibal and Joey remained silent.

"Aleluya, brothers. Amen!" Juan said.

"Amen!" said Josefo.

"Amen," said Serafina.

176

They waited and looked at the two boys.

"Amen," whispered Hannibal.

"Amen," echoed Joey.

"We have services on Wednesdays, Fridays, and Saturday evenings, from eight o'clock on. On Sunday, we have afternoon services from one to four, sometimes longer," said Juan. "We expect to see you there, brothers. The step you have taken is a great one, and the house of the Lord awaits you. Jesus blesses you both. Amen."

"Don't fail us, brothers. Remain saved and free," said Josefo. "Amen."

"Be sure to come," said Serafina. "I will remind you if you forget." She smiled. "Amen."

They turned and walked down the block.

Hannibal and Joey looked at each other, and then at the small Bibles.

"Let's put these things away before someone sees us," said Hannibal. "We was lucky that Perry and Ralphy had split already, and didn't see that whole number they done on us."

Quickly, they put the Bibles into their loose-leaf binders.

"Joey," Hannibal asked, "do you think you can get over that chick?"

"Hannibal," Joey smiled, extending his right hand, "what chick you talking about?"

Hannibal slapped Joey's open palm. "All right!" he said.

They walked home and after a few blocks saw Ramona, Casilda, and Mary. They caught up with the girls.

"Hi," Hannibal called to them.

They all exchanged greetings, then walked along, talking

about school and some of the teachers. After a while, Ramona said, "Hey, Hannibal, I heard you and Joey turned into Aleluya people." Mary and Casilda began to giggle.

Joey looked at Hannibal wide-eyed.

"Where did you hear that?" he asked.

"Two little birds that seen you," Ramona answered, smiling.

"Oh, man," Hannibal said, "I was there only as the Savior. You see, it was a command performance. . . ." Hannibal paused and handed Joey his books. "Hold these." Everyone watched in amusement as he extended his arms. " 'Here I am,' I said. 'Them that wants to be saved must come to Papi.' " Hannibal turned and dipped, stepping to the left and to the right.

"Who you gonna save? Serafina?" Ramona asked.

Hannibal stopped for a moment and, looking at Ramona, he folded his arms. "You . . . Mami. . . . I'm gonna save you." He went toward her, extending his arms once more.

"Get out, silly," Ramona said, walking away from him. He continued to walk toward her.

"I'm gonna save you, Ramona Pérez. In spite of your sins and your ugly ways, you still worth saving."

They all laughed loudly as they watched Hannibal tease Ramona.

"Who's going to the dance at St. Anselm's next Friday?" asked Mary.

"I am," said Casilda.

"Me too," said Joey. "Hannibal," he called out, "you going to the dance on Friday, right?"

"Yeah!" answered Hannibal. "And I'm taking Ugly." He pointed to Ramona.

42 55

"We'll see about that, Hannibal. . . . You might wanna take Serafina instead," she said.

"Awww, come on, Ramona," Hannibal coaxed. "Come to the dance with me, O.K.?"

Ramona smiled at Hannibal and nodded. They both walked on ahead.